"I'd like to make a suggestion.

Ras had been weighing his larger idea ever since it occurred to him. This new brainstorm would be a way to try out a short version and if it didn't feel right, he wouldn't take it any further.

"What's that?" Gracie licked a drop of pancake syrup from the corner of her mouth. He hoped she'd do it again.

"Rather than following the exact itinerary of that bus tour tomorrow, possibly having to stay too long or leave too soon at any of the destinations, I've reserved a private car to drive me around Miami. Would you join me?" He realized that was an odd proposal coming from someone she'd just met yesterday. He wished he could assure her that his intentions were respectable. Because he'd only be with her for a short time before he boarded his yacht never to see her again, he thought it best not to reveal his identity. "As a travel agent, I'm sure you know the sights. In fact, can I hire you as my tour guide? I'll pay you for the day."

Dear Reader,

When I think about the romances I want to write about, sometimes their location becomes a guiding light. Maybe my couple's emotions thrive on the excitement of a glittering city. Or they need a beach at sunset in order to open their hearts. Or maybe it's the lush tropics where their love can grow along with the flora and fauna. Because Gracie and Ras were both running toward uncertain futures, I had the idea to keep them traveling. So, fasten your seat belts and join them on their wild odyssey from a cruise ship to a limousine to an airboat to a luxury yacht to a two-seater plane. The wheels are turning as they voyage into the love neither thought they'd arrive at.

Together, they ride the US Eastern Seaboard from Miami to New York, stopping in Savannah, Charleston, Washington, DC, and the Hamptons until they reach the end of their line in the Big Apple. What happens in between alters them as much as the leaves change color in early autumn.

I'm glad you're with me on this ultimate whisk-you-away journey of the miles and the heart.

Andrea xx

Adventure with a Secret Prince

Andrea Bolter

If you purchased this book without a cover you should be aware that this book is stolen property. It was reported as "unsold and destroyed" to the publisher, and neither the author nor the publisher has received any payment for this "stripped book."

HARLEQUIN®
Romance™

PLEASE RECYCLE • THIS PRODUCT IS RECYCLABLE •
Recycling programs for this product may not exist in your area.

ISBN-13: 978-1-335-40715-3

Adventure with a Secret Prince

Copyright © 2022 by Andrea Bolter

All rights reserved. No part of this book may be used or reproduced in any manner whatsoever without written permission except in the case of brief quotations embodied in critical articles and reviews.

This is a work of fiction. Names, characters, places and incidents are either the product of the author's imagination or are used fictitiously. Any resemblance to actual persons, living or dead, businesses, companies, events or locales is entirely coincidental.

For questions and comments about the quality of this book, please contact us at CustomerService@Harlequin.com.

Harlequin Enterprises ULC
22 Adelaide St. West, 41st Floor
Toronto, Ontario M5H 4E3, Canada
www.Harlequin.com

Printed in U.S.A.

Andrea Bolter has always been fascinated by matters of the heart. In fact, she's the one her girlfriends turn to for advice with their love lives. A city mouse, she lives in Los Angeles with her husband and daughter. She loves travel, rock 'n' roll, sitting at cafés and watching romantic comedies she's already seen a hundred times. Say hi at andreabolter.com.

Books by Andrea Bolter

Harlequin Romance

Billion-Dollar Matches collection

Caribbean Nights with the Tycoon

Her New York Billionaire
Her Las Vegas Wedding
The Italian's Runaway Princess
The Prince's Cinderella
His Convenient New York Bride
Captivated by Her Parisian Billionaire
Wedding Date with the Billionaire

Visit the Author Profile page at Harlequin.com.

For Ronna

Praise for
Andrea Bolter

"From that first book I was completely hooked with her stories and this is easily my all-time favorite to date. I thoroughly enjoyed this, it's the perfect little escapism."

—*Goodreads* on *Captivated by Her Parisian Billionaire*

CHAPTER ONE

"COME, SON, THE CAR is waiting to take us to the airport."

Ras had stopped walking after he and his father exited the Secretariat, the skyscraper building at the United Nations headquarters in New York. People were hurrying to and fro, and the numerous member flags flown in the plaza were billowing in the early autumn sunshine. Ras stared up at those flags for a moment. They waved in the freedom he was about to claim, still tethered to poles but allowed to flutter as the breeze took them.

The moment had arrived.

"Father, I'm not going home with you."

"Whatever are you talking about, Ras? You're to be married in less than two months."

"I shall be. But first, I'm going to spend some time on my own." The words fell out even easier than he'd expected them to. His conviction had been growing for weeks; years, really, in a certain way. Everything had been building to this point. And his plan had been in place well before they'd taken this trip to New York to attend a UN summit on global culture.

"Do not start with that nonsense again." Ras had brought this up previously with his father, who always dismissed him out of hand. Patiently waiting for the right time, Ras knew it was now or never. His father went on, "We don't want to miss our runway time." The private plane would have been given only a small window of minutes to take to the skies. His father was in a hurry. Ras, however, was not.

For once in his life, he was going to breathe at his own pace, and he took in a slow, clean inhale for emphasis. Yet this was not the spot to see his father off. So he gave a yank on the small wheeled case that his father would have assumed contained paperwork but, in fact, was filled with clothing and toiletries. He'd purchase more along the way.

Since they were to leave New York today, Ras's valet had packed his wardrobe into traveling cases and saw that they were loaded into cars going to the airport, as usual. Ras did nothing to stop the process and made a point of keeping the small case with him. Now tugging it behind him, he resumed striding with his father away from the UN Plaza toward their waiting limo. "Father, I want you to understand," he explained as they moved forward decisively, sharing the same pace, "I will return home well in time for my impending nuptials. I love you, and I will always love and honor the memory of my late mother. However, in order to be whole, I must experience choice. I need to wander a bit, to roam without formalities and handlers and bodyguards. You know that mother wanted that for me. She always told me as much."

His mother had indeed urged him many times that in order to fulfill his obligations, he needed to be content. She'd had a wanderlust that she'd passed on to her only child prior to her untimely death when Ras was fifteen. And fifteen years later, he was finally going to actualize that desire. For her and for himself.

"I've told you, son, that is too dangerous," his father insisted. "And, I might add, absurdly timed." Yes, Ras hadn't forgotten his arranged marriage to a woman he didn't love.

They reached the limo where the driver was awaiting their arrival, holding the door open. "I'll be safe. I promise you."

"Ras, get in the car. Stop behaving like a

child." His father slid into the limo seat. "You are bound by responsibilities."

"And I shall honor them. I'll be home in a few weeks. I'll stay in touch." He'd already purchased several untraceable cell phones for the purpose. He didn't want to cause his father worry. Yet this was something he had to go through with. "See you soon." He bowed with his shoulders before turning away from the limo.

"Go after him," he heard his father implore a bodyguard who was standing at attention nearby.

Expecting that as well, His Royal Highness Rasmayada, crown prince of Ko Pha Lano, a sovereign island nation in the Gulf of Thailand, maneuvered himself into the throngs of people surrounding the UN. Seeming to escape the bodyguard. In his fine wool but undistinguishable gray suit, Ras easily blended into the crowd. Leaving his father, His Majesty King Maho, to travel home without him.

Ras's heart pounded with exhilaration as he hurried this way and that through the streets away from the UN. He'd only been to New York and Washington, DC, on official occasions, conferences with dignitaries and meetings with politicians. Always chauffeured in cars with tinted windows, whisking him to private entrances. His plan today was easy to follow in the grid of Manhattan streets. The UN was at the East River and he was headed west to get to his destination at the Hudson River, the two bodies of water flanking the great metropolis.

Realistically, he knew that he likely hadn't fully escaped his father's surveillance. The king might employ top-notch security to locate Ras, possibly even cutting his scheme short. All the more reason he'd be sure to enjoy every moment of this time-out from the regimen of his life. In his thirty years he'd been respectful and proper, habits he had no intention of changing. Even down to marrying Her Royal Highness Princess Vajhana from the neighboring island of Ko Yaolum, a unification that was designed to combine the resources of the two nations to bring more much-needed employment and prosperity to their citizens. Vajhana was not a bride Ras would have picked for himself. While attractive and educated, she was also frivolous and petty. He'd already resigned himself to hoping for no more than an amenable partnership with her, one that would produce an heir to his eventual throne. He was not expecting passion and burning love although, secretly, he wished for what his parents had. Until the loss of his wife had turned his father into a brittle shell.

Once he'd cleared away from the UN area Ras hailed a taxi, having only seen the practice done in movies. The driver wore a turban, and the inside of the car had an artificial pine smell. As they chugged through stop-and-go traffic, horns honked and drivers yelled out their windows to curse at each other. Ras appreciated every second of being in the center of the real New York and would return to explore lesser-known parts of the city at the end of his journey. At that point, hopefully no one would be looking for him.

He hardly knew where to focus his eyes as they passed through the Times Square area. Not quite as large and pulsing as Tokyo's Shibuya Crossing, nonetheless, the bright lights of the jumbotron advertisements, the Broadway theaters, oversize stores and street vendors were teeming with activity. Continuing west, the driver brought him to his destination at the port terminal. He paid the fare and got out of the cab. Toting his wheeled case, he took in the sheer size of the cruise ship he was about to board, the vessel itself aptly named *Liberation*. It had the capacity to hold three thousand passengers, not large by cruise standards but compared to the private yachts on which Ras traveled, it was enormous.

At home in the palace when he began finalizing his design for this trip, a travel website had featured information about this newly completed ship. The maiden voyage of uber-luxury Carat Cruises' newest addition to its fleet would begin in New York, heading toward its destination of Miami, a short distance meant to showcase the lavish amenities onboard. The passage was perfect for getting Ras away from New York unnoticed. No one would suspect a crown prince to be traveling on a public cruise. Then, instead of returning to New York, he had a yacht waiting for him in Miami. When he disembarked there presumably for a day of sightseeing, he simply wouldn't return to the cruise ship.

The brisk air of the waterfront filled his lungs as he strode up the gangway to board, bluffing to the porters that his luggage had arrived separately and checking in merely his small case. He didn't proceed directly to his stateroom suite. Instead, he remained on deck to watch when the ship left the shore.

"Ladies and gentlemen, this is Captain Batista," a voice boomed through the loudspeakers stationed at various points on the deck where

many of the passengers had gathered after embarking. "On behalf of the crew and everyone
at Carat Cruises, welcome to *Liberation*!"

"That's something," Gracie Russo said to herself as much as to anyone as the ship left the
dock. It was sometimes hard to believe that
Manhattan was actually an island. With its
millions of residents and twenty-four-hours-a-
day verve, it had always felt to her like a small
country, one that she'd traveled to many times
by bus and train. But from the vantage point
of a cruise ship on the Hudson, the great skyscrapers and architectural marvels were indeed
surrounded by bodies of water.

"It is, at that." Obviously, Gracie's comment
was loud enough to be heard. As *Liberation*
turned to chart its way toward the heart of the
Atlantic Ocean, Gracie side-eyed the baritone
that had spoken to her. The voice belonged to
a tall and attractive man gazing at the island as
they left it. "The Manhattan buildings always
look to me like important and purposeful men."

His expensive suit struck her as a rather formal choice for the cruise's departure. Perhaps
he was an important and purposeful man himself. He certainly looked excellent in his outfit's tailored fit. Gracie wore a flowered dress

and carried a cardigan in case the sea breeze brought a chill. The leaves would be changing color to welcome autumn literally any day now.

"Is this your first time seeing the city from the water?" she asked, angling to face him.

"Yes, exactly. I've only flown in, so the perspective is quite different."

Gracie was interested in the points of view of some typical cruise passengers. Although this man seemed anything but typical with an accent that suggested elite schooling and that gray suit, white shirt and charcoal tie. His skin was tan and his eyes dark; prominent cheekbones and a razor-sharp jaw added up to a stunningly fine face. She couldn't help but wonder if he was on the ship alone as there was no companion in sight. What would a man like him be doing alone on a ship? Compelled to continue the chitchat she asked, "Do you cruise often?"

She'd been learning all about cruise culture, about people who preferred that mode of travel with its all-inclusive accommodations, dining options, port excursions and carefully customized itineraries. In fact, Gracie had been learning about all types of tourism and leisure. Because she was finally going to fulfill her dream of becoming a luxury travel consultant. Truth be told, just as *Liberation* had embarked so had she. This was her maiden voyage as an industry professional. She was nervous and excited all at once.

The handsome passenger rotated his long neck slowly, very slowly, from left to right, scanning the entire vista both on the cruise ship's deck and even past it to the small boats that also rode the river. It somehow didn't seem like he was looking for anyone in particular among the many passengers who had gathered on deck to watch the departure from port. Yet his heavy eyebrows furrowed, as if he was suspicious, maybe even in danger. She couldn't imagine what someone would be worried about when they'd just set sail on a pleasure cruise, something she'd never done. Of course, his reasons were none of her affair. Satisfied, at least momentarily with his investigation, he returned his gaze to Gracie. The depth of his gaze ran right through her, forcing its way into every vein. There was something very compelling about this man. She was glad he was nothing to her but a stranger on a deck, as the last thing she needed was any entanglements when she had finally set herself free in every way. He rounded back to her original question. "Public cruises, no. I do travel quite a bit by yacht, though."

Of course, he did. He was almost out of place on this ship, despite the fact that it was touted as being ultra-luxurious in every detail and was the newest vessel in Carat's fleet, the most exclusive cruise line in the world. This man was somehow beyond even that.

"Where are you from?" Gracie inquired, rationalizing that the question was still within the realm of superficial banter fellow passengers would have.

He scoped out another panorama before saying succinctly, "Asia." She'd have guessed as much from his features, but the full stop on the end of his answer let her know that she was not going to get a longitude and latitude any more specific than that.

A moment later, snapping back from that bird's-eye survey he'd taken, he asked, "Yourself?"

She gestured with her head to the other side of the Hudson River, to the land it bordered on the opposite side from Manhattan. "New Jersey. Born and raised." If a person could call the sorry excuse for parenting she'd received *raised.* Not to mention what had gone on between *born* and the ripe old age of twenty-six. He'd have been able to guess from her bargain cotton dress that she didn't live on Park Avenue.

"Ah, so you must know the US Eastern Seaboard like the back of your hand?"

She'd lived in three places, all in New Jersey. Born in a seedy outskirt of the capital city, Trenton. Then she'd moved to the shore at Point Pleasant, whose name was a matter of opinion, with her biggest mistake, named Davis. And for the last two years she'd been in the north of the state, in Newark. Not exactly the pounding pulse of urbanity but close to New York. As to the rest of the East Coast, she knew of all the places she intended to visit so that she could advise clients. She hoped to make *nowhere* her new home, done being left behind, done being at the mercy of others, done holding anything dear because it would surely be taken from her. She had it all mapped out. She'd be the perpetual wanderer, financing her own ride with the money she made planning other people's.

"My whole life fits into four boxes," she'd said to Jen yesterday as she'd lifted them into her friend's already cramped Staten Island apartment, which, like New Jersey, was not the most coveted address in the New York area.

"Down to the essentials," Jen had commended her.

"Thank you for agreeing to keep my stuff and letting me have my mail sent here, too."

"Live your dream."

Gracie swiped the hair that had fallen into her eyes when she was carrying the boxes. "Let's hope so."

"Think of all the exotic and interesting people you'll meet," Jen had said. "Maybe even *men* people."

"Oh, you know there'll be no more of that for me. I'm a solo voyager."

Funny that Jen had been right about the interesting men, having just met one. Although he was none of her concern. "This cruise is more an introduction to the ship than a tour of the eastern US," she mentioned in case he didn't already know. "It only ports in Miami."

"Yes, I know. I'm only planning ahead to—" he abruptly reworked his own thought "—see the sights someday."

Potential client? Would it be too bold of her to give him a business card? Business card. Gracie Russo was a businesswoman. She'd studied as many popular locations as thoroughly as she could, taken courses in tourism and become certified, and learned all of the latest software programs. She'd been hired on a freelance basis by a cooperative of travel agents. The only money she'd make would be on commission, so she was going to have to work hard and make a name for herself.

She'd versed herself in all things Carat Cruises, which had held a reputation for decades as being the absolute finest. What she hadn't yet amassed were the funds to personally visit all of the travel destinations she would be selling to clients. But she had to start somewhere. Which was why when she'd read on an industry website that a limited number of travel professionals were being invited to take *Liberation*'s maiden voyage so that, no doubt, they could recommend it, Gracie jumped at the chance. Her former job as a cashier at a bus station in Newark qualifying her as a travel professional might have been a stretch. Although it was technically travel-related, wasn't it? And she was now a member of the agency co-op even though she hadn't had any bookings yet.

When she'd strode up the gangway to board a little while ago, an electric charge fired through her as she followed the check-in signs for Tourism Professionals. Her bags portered to her stateroom, she was warmly welcomed at the reception table that held no more than a list of names. She wasn't questioned about her credentials despite her trepidation that she might have been. An extensive color brochure of the ship's amenities and the numerous activities planned would await her in the stateroom, although she'd already studied it in great detail online.

It was her moment. When the cruise returned to New York after its four-day voyage, her online travel agency would be open for business. Next, she'd planned a rental car trip through New England to see the fall colors and investigate the bed-and-breakfast inns whose owners had offered travel agents complimentary accommodations to come tour their properties. With enough money diligently saved to keep her for a few months before a first commission was earned, she was filled with gusto at the future she'd been waiting for, for far too long. Okay, she was in equal measure terrified.

What if none of it worked out? she suddenly thought in a moment of panic. She'd given up her job and her apartment. It was no-holds-barred *go for it* time. Well, she mused, if it all fell apart, it wouldn't be the first time a promise didn't come true. What did she have to lose at this point?

"*Liberation* guests." The captain's voice came through the loudspeakers once again. "We'll begin our welcome festivities shortly, but let me first turn your attention to that grand monument known the world over."

The closer they approached, the larger the three-hundred-foot Statue of Liberty appeared. Although Gracie had spent her life nearby, she would never tire of seeing Lady Liberty's oxidized copper-green glory.

"Indeed, a symbol the whole world understands," said the elegant stranger still standing next to her, who was himself studying the details of the magnificent representation of a Roman goddess. For no comprehensible reason, she wished his eyes were intently on her instead of on Liberty.

Gracie glanced around at the passengers on the deck. With Carat's clientele, her shipmates were likely to be among the most privileged people on the planet. Those who demanded, and received, the best of everything. Yet she couldn't help but see a bit of wonder in all of their eyes as they took in the majesty of the statue. "Did you know that her crown has seven spikes in acknowledgment of the seven continents and the seven oceans of the world?" Gracie hoped to visit them all someday.

"Ladies and gentlemen, I am Aston, your cruise director," a strapping man with red hair and an

Australian accent announced through a hand-held microphone as he bounced onto the deck. "As we say goodbye to New York for a few short days, Carat Cruises has a surprise." He was accompanied by other members of the crew who dispersed to shake hands and give individual greetings to dozens of passengers. They all had big smiles and donned crisp blue shirts embroidered with the Carat diamond logo, both the male and female members wearing them tucked into fitted slacks. Smartly casual but polished. In the small bag he'd brought, Ras had a couple of leisure outfits other than the overdressed suit he was wearing, which he worried made him look conspicuous. He'd been in full royal regalia for the meetings at the UN and in suits for dinners.

Aston continued, "We hope to have your every wish fulfilled onboard *Liberation* with her state-of-the-art facilities. To kick things off, we're celebrating the rich culture of our port city, Miami, with a very special guest. You know her as one of Cuba's best-known singers. She's toured the planet with her renowned band, selling out arenas in over forty countries. Topping both the pop and Latin music charts for over a decade. Let's give a big Carat

Cruises welcome to eleven-time Grammy winner, Benita Diaz!"

Ras heard audible gasps from a few people. Benita Diaz was a global superstar. No one would have expected her to be entertaining on this short cruise. A massive smile crossed the pretty face of the woman in the flowered dress he'd been talking to, whose name he still didn't know. "Ah, a brilliant publicity move," she extolled. A bubbly energy sparked off her. He had no idea why, but he took one step closer to her. Then thought better of it and retreated. She observed his faux pas but continued. "Everyone will be posting and talking about this!" He didn't know why Carat Cruises' public relations would be of interest to her. But she radiated a contagious enthusiasm His Royal Highness, sometimes thinking of his title as being something outside of himself, wasn't used to being around. He lived behind a window of propriety and control.

Her comment that people would be posting about this unexpected celebrity appearance caused Ras to scan the deck once again. Cell phones and cameras were trained on the entertainment storming the deck. There was always the possibility of Ras being recognized by the general public. He tried to reassure himself the crown prince of a very small nation halfway around the world was not likely to be noticed aboard this tourist cruise. Yet somehow, with paparazzi seeming to sprout up from under the surface of the earth, his photo did occasionally land on websites and magazines that catered to those obsessed with young royals. His flashy bride-to-be was frequently photographed at the world's biggest parties, a slave to fashion and the famous. He had always been cognizant of poise and dignity so there had never been anything tawdry the media could uncover about him. Nonetheless, every couple of years he'd been chosen as one of the world's most attractive princes or another similarly embarrassing moniker.

In any case, as a line of men in white bearing horn instruments and handheld drums began to play, Ras was sure there were no eyes on him. Cuban tempos and percussion spread across the deck, garnering everyone's attention. *"Bienvenidos!"* a female voice boomed through a microphone over the music. Dancers with long legs and colorful feathery costumes sashayed into position and began their choreography to the lively music. Then their line parted in half to welcome Benita Diaz in a sparkling red dress with massive ruffles. She bounded out almost as if from a cannon blast. "Welcome. To. *Liberation!*"

The passengers applauded and hooted. Ras glanced at the woman still beside him who began bobbing her head in time with the music. The afternoon sun glinted off her golden hair, which fell in loose waves to her shoulders. She was certainly attractive, Ras admitted in his mind. Which gave him a wicked rush he wanted more of. No wonder his subconscious made him take that step forward toward her. Thank goodness the rational part of his brain had immediately retracted the error. This personal voyage wasn't a premarital stag party. It was his own company he wished to keep.

As Benita tore into one of her most popular songs, it seemed everyone on deck cut loose and either shimmied their shoulders or wiggled their hips to the rhythm. Except him, of course. The media might choose to portray him as one of the world's most eligible royals, but while he had certainly enjoyed the company of women, he was not a playboy. His parents had taught him decorum and respect for the honor of leading a nation. His Royal Highness Rasmayada of Ko Pha Lano most certainly did not *shake his booty*. In public, anyway. That didn't stop him from enjoying the sight of the silky shoulders next to him as they shimmied.

"I love this song!" the owner of the shoulders exclaimed.

"What's your name?"

"Gracie Russo. Yours?"

"Ras." He wouldn't say more. As a matter of fact, he should have given her a phony name. Well, probably no harm so far, he told himself. A reminder that while this Gracie was friendly, he was traveling incognito and couldn't forget it.

"Nice to meet you." She flashed a smile at him that made a squiggle flitter up his spine. His shoulders arched sharply.

After Benita, her dancers and her band played several of their hits in a set that lasted about half an hour, they left the deck to thunderous applause.

Cruise Director Aston took to the mic again. "We're glad you enjoyed our *special* guest. Now we'd like to turn your attention to our coffee reception where you can sample a cup of good old New York regular and a rich Café Cubano. The brews are ready and waiting!"

Gracie turned around as did Ras to see the buffet tables set with cups, and decorated with cuttings from coffee trees, including the cherries that contained the beans. There were trays full of cookies and chocolates for the taking. Guests began making their way toward the offerings. She placed her hand on his upper arm by way of gesture. "Let's go get some."

He was unused to being touched and instinctively pulled back. After all, a prince had handlers surrounding him at all times in public, as much as a barricade as anything else. Although there was no way Gracie's soft pull could have meant him any harm, and he missed the feel of her as soon as he'd ended it. She gave him a quizzical look. Perhaps his retreat was startling to her. Especially after he'd taken a step closer to her earlier. He tried to cover his slip with, "Yes, we must try the coffees."

"Sounds great."

Even though they were among the elite on this exclusive cruise, Ras was surprised at the mad rush toward the buffet. He was sure the crew knew exactly how much refreshment to prepare and wasn't in danger of running out. Cruise culture, he noted to himself. He wasn't accustomed to being in a crowd other than when he passed through them in an official capacity, with both liveried and undercover protection. He was glad that in a couple of days, he'd be picking up his private yacht in Miami.

Looking over at Gracie, though, he had this completely unprovoked notion that he'd be sad alone. Which, since he'd exchanged nothing more than a few words with her and spoken to no one else in the last hour, was simply ridiculous. Although when her caramel eyes met his for an unspoken moment of connection, something in his spirit soared. "About that coffee…" He snapped out of it to square himself and get back to business.

"This is very cute," Gracie said, surveying the buffet table once they reached it. "See these blue-and-white coffee cups with the Greek key design on them? Those cups used to be the kind every place in New York that sold coffee had before the brand-name coffee shops took over. Made of paper, of course. These are porcelain."

"What's a regular coffee?" Ras asked, having never heard the term.

"Milk and sugar already mixed in."

"Ah, yes, New York. No fussing around."

"Let's get serious about these sweets." She took one of the small plates provided and handed one to Ras. Only a cool whisper of air separated her fingers from his as he took it. He smiled as she helped herself to one of each and every of the offerings, double-checking that she hadn't missed any. There were shortbreads half dipped in chocolate. Cherry chocolate chip cookies. Chocolate cookies bursting with nuts. Biscotti. Macarons. Cuban sugar cookies. Then assorted filled chocolates as well as squares. It was a chocolate festival. "Ooh, did I get that dark chocolate oval?" She pointed.

"Yes, Gracie, I think you've thoroughly loaded your plate," he said with an exuberant laugh so unlike him. At first, he only took one each of three selections. But then, carried away by her devotion, he piled his plate just the same as hers, feeling like a greedy child at a candy shop, an experience he'd never actually had.

You only live once.

"We need our Café Cubanos."

"What type of preparation is that?"

"It's basically an espresso with sugar." Served in small cups that were brown on the outside and white inside, the frothy brew smelled utterly intoxicating. He took a tray from a stack provided. Placing the four coffees and the two overflowing plates on it, he felt like a teenager holding books for a cute girl. It elicited a sort of pride that he didn't get often, as mundane things such as this were done for him. The tray also confirmed that they headed together toward an empty table to sit at.

He stopped, tray in hand.

"Is something wrong?" she asked.

What on earth was he doing? He had no idea who this woman was. A prince didn't suddenly keep company with someone he'd met on a cruise an hour ago. Most definitely not an engaged prince. He and Vajhana had been matched by their fathers and had agreed from their very first meeting that they would put no monogamy claims on each other. Yet that didn't mean he'd abandon his usual discretion when having his occasional liaisons with women. Which did not include the open deck of a public cruise.

Ras hadn't planned to actually talk to anyone on the ship. The cruise was just a mode of transportation to reach the yacht. In fact, he'd considered having all of his meals brought to his stateroom. It was unorthodox enough that he didn't get on that plane back to the island with his father. That he'd carefully planned this sojourn to explore on his own, to experience just a taste of life outside the palace walls. To escape being a prince for brief interludes as his mother had wanted him to, and told him so when he was a teenager before she died. To learn to be simply a man with his time his own, to know what that was like. He surely couldn't have imagined sharing a snack on a public deck with a beautiful young woman. Yet, blame it on the music, blame it on the coffee or blame it on Gracie's infectious smile. It turned out Ras's freedom quest had already begun.

CHAPTER TWO

"Oh, my gosh, have you tried the piece with nuts on top?" Gracie gestured to Ras's plate while he took a sip of his New York regular, light and sweet and smooth. She was referring to one of the chocolates in the black, pleated paper cups they'd put on their plates to sample. "It's heavenly."

Ras examined his plate. He located the confection she was referring to and studied it in his fingers. The top was studded with finely chopped almonds and sprinkled with slivers of sparkle. "The gold leaf is a nice touch."

"If you hold it a certain way, the sun glints off it. Perfect for outdoors."

"A little work of art, in and of itself." Ras couldn't say he'd ever given that much thought to an individual piece of candy. Although he did turn it right to left, forward and back, just to see the reflections. Had he been eat-

ing chocolates at an official function, neither
His Royal Highness nor whomever he was in
company with would have thought to admire
the creativity involved. *Thank you, Mother*, he
thought, silently lifting his eyes to the skies.
This was a perfect example of what she wanted
for him. For him to know small pleasures. To
serve himself a plateful of desserts without caring whether that was proper royal conduct. To
daydream, to imagine *what-if* with regard to
anything that came to mind. She'd believed it
would make him a better leader, more complete and able to see the world from perspec-
tives other than his own.

It was the kind of thing she and his father
did, every so often. Yes, they were role mod-
els to an entire nation and never took an action
that would be disrespectful of their positions.
At the same time, Queen Sirind had made sure
her family knew what grass felt like under their
feet and what it was to care for their beloved
Shih Tzu. It had been years since Ras thought
of Lucky, so named because Sirind had told
the dog daily what a fortunate destiny he had.
He'd died when Ras was thirteen, two years
before his mother. In retrospect, the family
should have immediately replaced Lucky with
another dog. That could have helped both him

and his father with their grief when Sirind died. It might have helped the king continue to have red blood running through his veins as opposed to the cold frame of a man he'd become.

In his mother's memory, he'd make sure his own children ran around the palace grounds and ate unreasonable amounts of sweets once in a while. And know of the real world. Biting into the chocolate he'd been watching catch the light, the milk chocolate robe gave way to a center of more almonds mixed with a buttery brittle that had both crackly and chewy bits.

"What do you think?" Gracie watched as he savored his bite.

"Yes, it is truly divine." He popped the rest of it in his mouth while she finished hers as well. Following that, he lifted his cup of Café Cubano. "What shall we toast to?"

"To…adventure."

"To adventure." They tapped their cups to each other's and sipped. "This coffee is perfect. Sweet enough to keep the bitterness from becoming too harsh."

"Is that a metaphor for life?"

He laughed at Gracie's observation. "I suppose you could say that."

"Have you tried the lemon macaron? I think that's my favorite so far."

Without hesitation, he put his onto her plate. "Please, have mine then."

She gave him a wistful look as if he'd just gifted her with fine jewels or something valuable. "That's so…thoughtful of you."

"It's just a sweet. There are probably more at the buffet table. Would you like me to get you some?" He was eager at the prospect, getting something for her that she wanted. Perhaps he'd watched too many movies and had a distorted view of how commoners flirted with each other. *Flirted?* Was he flirting with her? His Royal Highness didn't flirt.

Though the way she stared at him after his offer made him wonder if she'd been treated unkindly in the past, so dramatic was her gratitude for a macaron. Which made him curious about her. "No, thank you." Her voice went hardly above a whisper.

Was she on the cruise by herself? If she'd been with someone, wouldn't she be sharing heaven-sent chocolates with him? Or her? Or them? Would it be snooping to ask? It didn't matter, he figured. On a ship holding three thousand passengers, he'd likely never even see her past this interlude. "Are you traveling alone?"

"Yes," she said and then took a bite of the lemon confection. He waited for her to say more. She looked up to the sky with a hesitance he didn't understand. "For business. I'm a travel consultant. Carat Cruises invited a number of people in the industry for the voyage to introduce *Liberation*. No doubt in hopes we would recommend it to clients."

"A travel consultant. That must be interesting work."

"It will…it is."

"Perhaps you can offer me some recommendations. What would you suggest I see on the East Coast beyond the typical spots?"

"The East Coast covers a lot of ground. Savannah, Georgia, and Charleston, South Carolina are special places. Do you golf?"

"I do."

"Water sports?"

"Sure."

"Regional food?"

"Absolutely."

"You'll find it all, up and down the East Coast. You also might want to visit the Hamptons on Long Island, New York."

"Thank you for the tips." He flashed on an idea that was so impossible he forced his mind to dismiss it right away. "You said you were from New Jersey. What do you like in your home state?"

Was he imagining it or did her eyes mist up as she answered? "Getting out." Her gaze left his and went past the confines of the boat, out to the ocean and sky. Clearly, he'd touched a nerve. She flattened her palm to her stomach. After a few beats she seemed to remember that she was sitting with him. "There's nothing to see there."

She brought her attention back to her plate for another bite and onto another topic. "What do you do for work, Ras?"

It was a question he'd never been asked in his life. The words sounded so unusual. He decided not to answer the question at all. But then the silence became too awkward so he snapped, "I'm in a family business. We go back generations."

She lowered her head to her plate, lingering as she made her next selection, avoiding eye contact. Perhaps he came across as sharp, but his anonymity was crucial to this journey he had embarked on, so he wouldn't stand for being interviewed.

He tried to reengage, "What does *your* family do?"

Gracie barked out a laugh that was bitter and dark. "No one particular thing."

"How does that work?"

"It doesn't."

"What are they doing now?"

"I have no idea. I haven't talked to them in a while."

"You don't talk to your parents?"

"I don't know where they are."

"I'm sorry to pry. But that sounds like a difficult situation."

"It was. It's perfectly simple now."

While he and the king differed in their points of view about many things and had lost the closeness they'd had when Queen Sirind was alive, Ras couldn't imagine not talking to him even if they weren't in the same *business*. Gracie had obviously been through some trauma in her life. Ras's position meant he didn't really get to *know* people. He was mostly kept at a distance. At charity events, he might hear someone's troubles but the connection was never more than a few minutes long. He wondered what Gracie's heartaches and triumphs were.

Finally, when each and every sweet had been at least sampled if not devoured, he did a quick check to make sure no one appeared to be watching him. He'd never hear the details of Gracie's life. They were just two cordial strangers who'd crossed each other's paths for a brief repast. They'd never see each other again. As a matter of fact, he'd been out on deck and exposed long enough. It was time to say goodbye to her and retreat to his stateroom suite. His brows bunched at the idea even as he knew it was the right thing to do. He could continue to enjoy the sun, water and views from his private balcony.

"Well," he said as he pushed his chair back and stood, "this has been absolutely delightful, but I'd best be going. It was a pleasure to meet you, Gracie."

She seemed surprised at his abruptness and gazed up at him while still seated. Wow, were her eyes luminous? "Oh. Um… You, too."

He lowered his right hand to shake hers, another very unprince-like move as in his nation royals did not physically touch commoners, and he'd backed away when she'd tapped his arm earlier. He considered retreating again although that would be awkward since he instigated the contact. Plus, he had to admit to himself, he wanted to know what her hand felt like. The gesture afforded him the sensation of silk in human form as he was sure he'd never held anything as soft as her palm. Making a direct connection with those eyes, he knew the handshaking was really just an excuse not to let go of her fingers. He kept the moment one tick longer than he should have, maybe two, actually maybe three, knowing it was a once in a lifetime experience. Finally, his hand separated itself from hers, not without struggle, and he bowed his neck to her. "Thank you again for an enchanting kickoff to our passage. Enjoy the cruise."

"You too, Ras." As he walked away, the sound of her saying his nickname played over and over on a continuous loop in his brain. Ras. Not Prince Rasmayada. Not Your Royal Highness. Ras. *You too, Ras... Ras... Ras.* The tones in her voice were like music.

He reached his stateroom suite on the most exclusive deck of the ship, which he'd booked with the assumption it would be less trafficked. He swiped his key card, entered and removed his shoes, leaving them by the door. His small travel bag was almost silly in the spaciousness, but he lifted it onto the luggage bench. The enormous living room was centered by an L-shaped sectional sofa that faced the ocean on one side and a mounted television on the other. In front of it was a coffee table that had a nice stack of art books. A black table and chairs were set up for in-suite fine dining. A modern chandelier drew the eye up to the high ceilings. The far wall had a sliding glass door leading to a balcony with another table and chairs, plus chaise lounges. After surveying the equally well-appointed bedroom and master bath, he circled back to the living room and finally took off his suit jacket and tie. He undid the top button of his shirt and then sat down facing the water. Having left the balcony door open, he could hear the ocean waves and feel the sea air circulate in the room.

As he watched the waves of the Atlantic, he thought of oceans on the other side of the world. He realized, as if for the first time, how little time he spent alone. His day was often filled with meetings, many at his father's side. Evenings were generally spent at official or charitable functions, lately in the company of Princess Vajhana once their engagement had been brokered. He was genuinely humbled by the responsibilities his position brought, which would grow even more important when the crown sat upon his head. Leading his people was a great distinction. At the same time, the confines could be stifling. He needed this break away from Ko Pha Lano. Before he married and the particulars of being a husband, and hopefully a father, would define the next chapter of his life.

Out of his pocket, he retrieved one of the untraceable cell phones he'd purchased. Dialing a phone number known only to him and a very select few others, he heard the king's recorded greeting.

"It's Ras. As I told you in New York, I will come back in three weeks. I'm going to live out mother's wish for me. That, before I marry, I wander a bit. That I walk and think like a man not a royal." For example, boarding a public cruise ship and enjoying delicious treats eaten in the open air with a woman who had beautiful golden waves of hair. "To know what that is. Like you and she used to. I'm calling because I want to let you to know that I'm fine. I'll call again soon." With that, he tapped off the phone and tossed it beside him on the sofa.

Explore himself he did, as for the next couple of hours he stared out at the ocean, ideas coming to him one after the other. The status of the island. How when Sirind died it was not just a prince who'd lost his mother and a king who'd lost his wife. It was the whole nation who'd lost their queen. A loss that to this day it had never recovered from. The people of Ko Pha Lano needed their inspiration back. Spoiled and glamorous Princess Vajhana was not going to give that to them. Ras would need to do it himself. Even though he and his father didn't agree on the island's future. Perhaps his ultimate mission would be to change the king's mind.

His mother had been so right. He needed to see distant shores and have unfamiliar thoughts. Ideas were bouncing around his brain so fast he couldn't even catch them. That was okay. It was wonderful, in fact. But after he'd done enough brainstorming for the day, he couldn't bear to sit in his suite alone the rest of the day and evening. He decided to change the plan and take a walk around the ship.

"Oh, what are the odds?" Gracie choked out when she saw Ras heading toward her on the starboard side of the promenade deck.

Ras bowed his head. "Very unusual," he answered with a quick dart of his eyes right to left.

"Are you waiting for someone?" Had he ever said whether or not he was traveling alone?

"No, why? It's nice to see you again." He'd peered around several times during Benita Diaz's mini concert and again during the sweets buffet. She half expected to find out he was actually onboard with a wife or significant other and was trying to be sure he wasn't caught getting a little too friendly with another passenger. Although his big dark brown eyes held a gaze of trustworthiness. When he'd looked at her during their coffee chat, he fully looked. Giving her the impression she had all his interest. It was a nice feeling and something she was wholly unused to. In any case, the deep eyes were quite entrancing as she now encountered them for an unexpected second time.

"Where are you headed?" Solo travelers were rare, and it would be useful for her to know how this obviously well-to-do gentleman was going to spend his time onboard. Was he en route to the spa? The casino?

"I was going to peruse the boutiques." A shopper? She wouldn't have pegged him for one. She'd figured him as the type to have an assistant or perhaps even a personal tailor. She noticed that he still wore the same gray suit pants he'd been in when they'd first met. Although he'd taken off his tie and changed from a white shirt to a pale yellow one that was very becoming on him. Why wouldn't it be? He was six feet plus of lean muscle and the suit had fit to perfection, if not made specifically for him. Perhaps it was his posture, the way he carried himself, shoulders back, chiseled jaw just so, that made her certain he was successful and moneyed. "Where are you off to?"

"Just browsing around." After they'd finished their chocolates and coffee, he'd abruptly excused himself from the table. Gracie made her way to her stateroom and found the porter had left her luggage there as arranged. While it wasn't one of the ship's deluxe rooms, it was elegantly detailed. On the pillow of the king-size bed was a long-stem red rose with a ribbon tied around it that read *Welcome*. The bed linens were in the signature blue shades of Carat Cruises. On the nightstand were bottles of water.

Beyond the sleeping quarters was a dressing area. A large full-length mirror stood near the ample closet. While this introductory cruise was only for a few days, *Liberation* was intended for longer voyages. Passengers who chose fine dining and entertainment might have packed quite a bit of luggage filled with evening clothes. Gracie put the two nicer dresses she'd brought on hangers. A vanity table with a mirror and a chair was a handy place to get ready for wherever she was going on ship.

She took a minute to imagine having packed a trunk full of evening wear. Garments of fine fabric and fashionable style, clothes like nothing she'd ever worn. Next she envisioned opening up a large case filled with makeup and hair accessories. Dozens of shades of eye shadow and lipsticks to choose from, and her having the knowledge to apply it all so that it enhanced her features without overdoing it and looking cheap. Finally, she'd go to the stateroom's safe to pull out whatever jewels she'd brought along to complete her ensembles.

She laughed at her own reflection in the vanity mirror. It was nothing short of a miracle that she'd even gotten this far, finagling a complementary stateroom on an elite cruise ship. She hoped none of the staff would ever find out that working at a bus station didn't exactly qualify her as part of the tourism industry.

The travel professionals onboard were going to be given a full tour of the ascending levels of accommodations tomorrow. Gracie wanted to build a client base of luxury travelers because, of course, that would mean higher commissions. Plus she assumed there would be more opportunities like this one, for her to have the *whisk you away* experiences she'd been reading and watching videos about for her entire life. With parents who'd left her alone most of her life and then a boyfriend who might as well have, now she wanted to be the one leaving for here or there, not someone being left.

After freshening up, she'd stepped out to see all *Liberation* had to offer.

"Can I tag along with you?" she asked Ras, not wanting this coincidence to end. "I'd like to see the shops."

"Come with me?" He tilted his head as he considered her request, giving Gracie further reason to question whether he was trying to keep a secret. It was a simple yes or no question.

"Of course," he finally conceded and gestured with his hand for her to follow him. What sort of destiny had them crossing paths again on this enormous ship?

The first store they came upon sold items for use onboard. Bathing suits and cover-ups, pool shoes, T-shirts. "Do you want to go inside?" she asked.

"Yes, I don't have swimming attire."

"You didn't pack for water activities?"

"It's difficult to explain. Embarking on this cruise was…a sort of last-minute decision." He was a terrible liar. His eyebrows raised until they were flat lines, and those shapely full lips of his parted in a way that made him look thirsty. Earlier, he'd bristled when she'd asked about his *family business*. Oh, well, she figured, everyone had a story. What she did know about him was that when she'd taken his arm to lead him to the coffee buffet, he'd pulled away, uncomfortable at being touched. Although, later, he'd given her a prolonged handshake. And he'd carried their tray to a table so she had to follow. When she said the lemon confection was her favorite, he insisted she take his. She wasn't used to gentlemanly gestures and kindness like that. No one had ever noticed if something was her favorite. So her inner sense told her he was a good man even if he was obviously holding a mystery.

"The ocean is too cold to swim. Will you be going to the beach in Miami?"

"Beach, pool, I don't know. As I told you, I'll be traveling for a few weeks. Might as well be prepared for anything, right?"

If you can afford to, she thought to herself.

"Absolutely, you can never have too many options," she blurted and then felt silly at her phoniness. Truth was, she'd had the same bathing suit since she was eighteen.

While he perused the rack of men's swimwear, she surveyed the knickknacks and typical souvenirs, noting that they were more tastefully designed than usual. When she came across an infant onesie with a graphic design reading *Baby's First Cruise*, she winced. Instinctively, even after all this time, her hand reached to massage her belly. Would she do that forever? Now the motion had become a symbol of everything she'd lost. Hopefully, better times were ahead.

"Are you all right?" She hadn't noticed Ras come up beside her. "Are you seasick?"

Ah, he was reacting to her hand on her stomach. "Thank you, that's nice of you to ask." Davis would have never observed if she appeared unwell. He wasn't that kind of guy. "No, not seasick at all, just a silly habit."

After he paid for his selections he said, "I'm done here. I'm told there's a men's clothing shop a few doors down." As they made their way toward the exit, Ras turned in a certain way so as to block something behind him that, evidently, he didn't want her to see. Which, of course, only made her all the more curious. As they left, she did a quick swerve to see a book and magazine stand. Hmm. Was he famous, not wanting her to see him on a book or magazine cover? Was he an actor, a politician, was his *family business* a prominent one? If he was a famous face, wouldn't she, and other people, recognize him?

Nonetheless, it was fun to see the shopping gallery, and he led her past a luggage purveyor and a jewelry store to the men's shop. When they entered its quiet hush, the walls paneled with red wood, Gracie could tell the prices were going to add at least a zero to the end of any number she was used to. "I need casual clothes," Ras explained to the salesman who wore a jacket and tie.

"I can help you with that, sir." He nodded to Gracie. "Madam."

"Hi."

"Can you tell me a bit about your preferences, sir?" The question seemed to perturb Ras so the salesman went on. "For example, do you prefer a button-down shirt or would you like a polo style?"

Ras looked at him as if that was the most difficult decision he'd ever been asked to make. He thought about it for as long as he could before sort of giving up with a simple, "Yes."

Trying to make it easier, the salesman inquired, "For example, do you like chambray or would you prefer denim?"

"Do you have a personal stylist?"

"Of course, sir. Give me a moment to see if Charles is available." The salesman rushed back behind the sales floor to some private area.

"At home, I have a valet who manages my wardrobe," Ras told Gracie.

"Of course." She nodded as she tried to unpack that statement. He has a personal *valet*.

Who *manages* his wardrobe. If it needed confirming, obviously Ras was indeed wealthy. Not just well off. She'd guess dripping. And, as she'd learned at the first shop, possibly famous. This cruise was certainly getting off to an interesting start.

"Charles can assist you, if you'd like to follow me," the salesman said to him.

He seemed to consider the situation for a moment before asking, "Gracie, will you join me? That is if you don't have somewhere else to be."

"Sure." This could be instructive, to be allowed into the inner sanctum where the proverbial *haves* versus the *have nots* shopped. The salesman swiped a key card and ushered them into a salon. The room was painted ocean blue. Two rounded silver sofas formed a semicircle in front of a trio of tall mirrors that completed the circle, with a dais in the center.

A small-statured older man who wore fine suit pants, a shirt and tie with a measuring tape slung around his neck and a pin cushion on his wrist introduced himself as Charles. An attendant brought in a tray holding two glasses of champagne in tall flutes, offering one each to Ras and Gracie. They both accepted. "Madam, perhaps you'd like to sit down." Charles pointed to the sofas. Gracie sat on one of them, exquisitely comfortable. To Ras he said, "My associate tells me you'd like some assistance with casual items. May I take you to the dressing room and show you some selections?"

Ras sent a shrug and a smile to Gracie as he followed Charles, leaving her alone. Scanning the room, she saw a rack of clothes off to the side. Black tuxedos. One was a young child's size. Four more had emerald-colored cummerbunds and bow ties on each hanger at the ready. The last one on the rack was different. The cummerbund had black embroidery and a black border on the emerald fabric as did the tie, making it subtly but distinctly different from the others. Grace knew in an instant that she was looking at the menswear for a wedding. Getting married on a cruise was a popular choice. She'd imagine a ship like *Liberation* would have every possible detail needed for a world-class wedding.

She chewed her lip. Life could have gone in several different directions for her. She could have had parents who cared about her, given her the security to go after her dreams at an early age. She could have married a good man and had children. Or she could have married Davis. After he'd showed his true colors, she was glad she hadn't. He did her a favor by delivering the hurt before it was too late. Never even knowing what had happened afterward.

As a result of her past choices and those made for her, she knew who she was. She'd never form a *forever after* with anyone. Never take those vows. Not at a neighborhood church in New Jersey and not on an opulent cruise. She was sailing alone, on this passage and beyond. That was that.

Ras and Charles exited the dressing room. Well-fitting jeans showcased Ras's long legs and a pale pink button-down shirt worn untucked was just right for relaxed elegance. While he'd looked businessman-handsome in his suit, this outfit was more easy confidence, and extremely hot, actually. "You look…that looks…great," she said, stammering.

Charles brought him to the mirrors for tailoring adjustments. Once that was done he asked, "Madam, may we show you another ensemble?"

Gracie took a sip of her champagne. She wasn't expecting her freebie ticket on this cruise to already be so much fun.

With the clothes to be delivered to his suite, Ras stood outside the men's shop with Gracie. "Thank you. It was wonderful to have a woman's eye, not to mention a helpful second opinion. As I told you, my clothes are generally selected for me." It was an unexpected pleasure to have an attentive companion along with him. If he'd been in the same situation with his fiancée and they were shopping for him and not her, she'd have bided her time on her phone and never looked up.

"My pleasure, Ras. I've never seen a private salon like that so it was fascinating. I like what you picked." Her approval made him happy in an unexplainable way.

"Well, I've kept you long enough." Once again he was to bid her farewell and, given the three thousand other passengers onboard, was unlikely to see her yet again. He fought his vocal cords from asking to. Spending time with people was not part of his trip's itinerary. He merely wanted to try being without his rigid schedule and expectations. He hadn't contemplated this voyage having anything to do with a woman. Although, he was drawn to Gracie. She had spirit and verve so unlike his interactions at the palace. It had been fun enjoying the concert and gorging on those delicious sweets, with her enthusiasm heightening the experience. That strange thought took hold again, but he knew he had to reject it. Instead, a few simple words choked out of his throat. "Goodbye, then. It's been a pleasure."

"Have a great rest of your trip." She gave him a genuine smile that shot like a beam right into his heart, sending a warm sensation to his chest that he wasn't sure how he'd get by without when it wore off. As she turned and headed away from the shopping area, he commanded himself not to watch her walk. That was, he meant to. Instead, his eyes took a slow slide from the honeyed strands of her hair, the cut of her dress and down to the shapely legs that carried her away from him.

After she was out of view, he strolled through another of the shopping lanes, one an enormous Carat Cruises office busy with people gathering information and perhaps booking for future sailings. Ras saw the glossy advertisements on the walls and knew he'd never cruise to Nova Scotia or down to the Caribbean on a vessel like this. His decree was set, and he was very fortunate indeed to be born into the humbling responsibility of the welfare of his subjects. It also afforded him almost every luxury possible. Except that of living as a common man. While he knew it was self-centered and something he'd need to work through by the time the crown sat on his head, Ras had been plagued by loneliness after his mother died. Partially it was because his father had also died, figuratively, along with her. There was no joy in the palace without her in it. He had no genuine intimacy with anyone. Certainly not with his intended, who he barely knew but didn't like. Vajhana was a quintessential party princess, a breed he'd never had interest in. Plus they'd been clear with each other about what they did, and didn't expect from their preordained marriage. Real intimacy was unlikely.

Ras did rendezvous with women occasionally. High-ranking career women who knew that a weekend with him at a private resort or on an adventure sport trip meant nothing more than a getaway. Even those excursions had grown tiresome. His mother was the only one he'd laughed with. Appreciated little things with. In her company he could be silly, say anything and truly be himself.

As Ras passed a toy store, he smiled wistfully when two parents presented a young boy, presumably their son, with a large replica of *Liberation*. It had human figurines that moved and doors that opened. A splendid souvenir. Would Ras playing with his own child someday fill up the hole that was left when his mother died?

And was it a crime, or even a surprise, that he already missed Gracie's company? He wondered where she was going. Perhaps to lay by the pool. Maybe she was taking a painting class or having a massage. Ras absolutely did not envision Gracie in a spa robe untying the belt and letting the thick terry cloth sides fall open to reveal her no doubt creamy skin underneath. He snickered at himself, at the mere thought of that.

When he passed the entrance to the casino, he noticed two Asian men wearing black suits. Was he imagining it, or were they staring at him? He knew from the minute he didn't get into the car with his father at the UN there would be a good chance that His Majesty would have his son followed. Deeming his son's grand scheme too risky to be left alone. For all he knew, half a dozen members of a security detail could have trailed him across Manhattan's Midtown and gotten onboard with him. His eyes darted to a woman in line at the casino cashier who smiled at him. So did another sitting at one of the slot machines. He suddenly felt claustrophobic.

"Would you like to do some gaming, sir?" a crew member asked. He glanced at the Carat

Cruises insignia on the chest of her blue blazer. She startled him out of his web of suspicion.

"No. No, thank you."

"Let us know if you change your mind. One of our casino concierges would be glad to explain any of our games if you're unfamiliar with them. We feature baccarat, roulette, blackjack, craps and poker." Ras had visited the most posh and high-stakes casinos in the world and was adept at all of the games.

But this cruise was just a means of transportation to the yacht in Miami. He wasn't planning to participate in any of the *Liberation*'s activities where he'd be highly visible. After the ship departed, he'd got carried away with Gracie and with delectable chocolate. He'd be wise to bide his time from here on hidden in his stateroom suite until they got to port. He hoped if he was, in fact, being shadowed he'd be able to evade the detail at that point. The smart move for the moment was to return to his suite and order dinner in.

When he got back, the new clothes were nicely hung in one of the closets, the selected shoes and leather jacket at the ready. Feeling that he must, he texted Vajhana that he'd been called away on a charitable mission and would see her soon. There was no response. Pouring himself a glass of water, he ruminated on what it might be like for two people to return each other's texts the moment they arrived, as if receiving word from the other was the highest priority. He didn't have that kind of relationship with Vajhana and never would. Hopefully, they could become co-parents who formed a pact to do right by their children and their subjects. That was all that was required. Nothing more. They'd even agreed that fidelity would not be part of their agreement.

So why was Ras so listless as he stared out at the vast ocean on which he sailed? Was it more than wanderlust that compelled him to undertake this quest? He thought of that boy in the toy shop, excited about the plastic ship model that was about the size of his torso. Ras vaguely remembered being that age, happily playing with toys on the palace lawn as if it were a typical backyard. Where his two parents would often sit down on the grass and join in. In love with each other and with their son. All the smiling left when Sirind died. It was as if she took the sunshine with her. Was he here to find it once again?

After watching the waves for a long, long time, it dawned on Ras why he'd thought so much about his mother since he'd boarded the ship. She'd wanted this for him, all but instructed him to make sure to retain something of his true self before the palace demanded all his allegiance and all of his time. Yet there was another reason he was wistful and nostalgic. It was meeting Gracie. She was vibrant and riveting. She made thick red blood run through his veins in a way it never had before.

Although he'd scanned the ship's QR code to order dinner, he just as quickly put his phone down. Hiding alone in his suite would be unbearable. He'd take a chance that he'd just been overly cautious when he'd thought those people at the casino knew who he was. What he'd do was drop into one of the informal and crowded restaurants on the ship, no need for dinner attire. Maybe he'd read a book or even play a relaxing video game. Just a regular guy having a bite to eat.

CHAPTER THREE

IN A COUPLE of the ship's casual restaurants, passengers were welcome to seat themselves. All Gracie cared about was getting a window table as, to her, that was the point of being on a ship. To never forget being on the water. To take in the sheer splendor of eating while traversing oceans and seas, to watch the life of the water, to see vistas of sunrise, sunset and the cycle of the moon. It was a bit late for dinner. The afternoon dessert and coffee spread had been quite filling. So by the time she was hungry again, the moon shone high in the sky with a bright hue illuminating the ebb and flow of the waves. It was a lovely sight.

Scanning the dining room, she realized that she wasn't the only one who wanted a table with a view. All of them were full. She noted a few tables throughout the dining room where only one person sat and wondered if they were traveling alone like she was. A sneaky smile crossed her lips when she thought of her chance encounters with Ras, both as an intriguing companion with whom to stuff her face with sweets, and then later to find herself in a private salon watching him model clothes and ask her opinion of them. What a strange circumstance that was, exciting with a forbidden feel that still had her buzzing. It wasn't every day she was in the company of people who could afford clothes like those let alone be allowed into the world of shopping for them. Piece by piece the stylist built outfits for him, each intended for certain occasions. For example, if Ras was to eat in this casual dining room right now perhaps he'd be in that medium brown blazer that so complemented his big brown...

She spotted the blazer first. When he turned his head she could see that it was indeed Ras, doing his usual scan of the room. The odds were so slim that she'd run into him another time, yet there he was! Her heart fluttered a couple of extra beats when he noticed her and a radiant smile swept across his handsome face. No one had ever looked that happy to see her. Was it meant to be that she'd come down to eat right at that moment? "We meet again," she sighed to herself.

He, of course, had one of those coveted window tables kissed by the moon's light. There was no reason not to share it. Not to mention that the prospect made her skin tingle. She maneuvered her way across the dining room in order to reach him. "We are on the same wavelength. Or is it that we ate so much chocolate earlier that we needed the same amount of recovery time?" she teased.

"I'm hungry now," he proclaimed. "What about you?"

"Yes!"

"You look lovely, by the way."

"Thank you." She mashed her lips at the compliment. Knowing she wasn't dressed for one of the formal dining experiences, she was still well put together in a fitted black skirt and a red blouse with a scooped collar that came to a bow on one side. If she had to interact with anyone professionally, she wouldn't be an embarrassment. Her pearl earrings, which she'd bought herself for her twenty-sixth birthday and were the only *real* jewelry she owned, would be her adornment for everything she wore on this cruise. There was no jewel case in her room's safe. But with her black kitten heels she felt chic. Chatting with a sophisticated man on a classy cruise was a far cry from foraging for food when she was a teenager and her parents, who had left her alone, failed to send her money for groceries. After one of his pauses in which he seemed to be weighing options he said, "Join me."

An open bottle of red wine sat on the table next to one half-filled glass. "Would you like a glass of Pinot Noir? Or something else to drink?" Ras asked as he waved a server over.

"Wine would be nice."

"Another glass, please," Ras requested. A corner of his mouth tipped, making Gracie feel like they were in on a secret. "It seems I have a guest." The server pulled a menu card from his apron and placed it on the tablecloth in front of Gracie.

"Did you already order?"

"Not yet."

"What looks good?" Besides him.

"I was thinking of starting with the Vidalia onion tart. Then the herb-crusted salmon with black rice."

"I was toying with the onion tart but the sweet pea soup with quail egg sounds amazing. I'll have the salmon, too." Ras relayed the order when the server came.

"Tomorrow, the travel industry group is going to be given a full tour, including all the dining options."

"What led you to become a travel agent?"

"I've been studying destinations around the world since I was a child." Maybe someone would suppose that she'd done a lot of traveling, and that's what prompted her to pursue it as a career. That wasn't her case, but better late than never. The appetizers were served. Her pea soup was a brighter green than she'd expected, not the sludge that typically came from a can, and it was sweet and fresh with that rich quail egg as an unusual garnish. "This is delicious. Would you like to taste it?" Funny that she felt absolutely comfortable offering him her food. They'd already shared a lot together, what with the chocolate and his personal fashion show. And without censoring herself, she'd told him a little about her parents. It must have been the anonymity of their acquaintanceship that gave her license. After they parted, he'd go off to his well-to-do life and his *family business*. And she'd go forward with hers, uncomfortable history like a piece of luggage she'd always tote around.

Watching him tip a spoon into her soup did seem intimate. And she couldn't help but study him as he brought it to his mouth, those full lips parting. How did he manage to make a spoonful of soup look so sexy?

"Ever since I was a young girl, I used to look at books and watch videos and TV shows that took place in the four corners of the earth," she babbled, unable to stop. "I couldn't get enough of dreaming about faraway locales. And I knew that I would see every spot someday. Beautiful lands with beaches or big fast cities, as long as they were very far from New Jersey." It was those goals of seeing the world, of being out from under the dysfunction of her household that kept her strong. When she was cold. When she was hungry. When she was scared. And her plans helped her carry on after Davis had mangled her life.

He tilted his head to study her, maybe to judge her. There was nothing she could do about that. She was who she was. But he simply raised his wineglass in a toast. "To adventure."

"To adventure." Apparently, that was their motto. They clinked and took a sip. "Do you travel a lot?"

"Yes. Although as I had mentioned, I've spent very little time on the Eastern Seaboard save for New York and Washington, DC. My mother loved to travel."

"She doesn't anymore?"

"She died. When I was fifteen."

"Oh, Ras, I'm sorry to hear that. Was she sick?"

She could hear a little catch in his throat before he answered. "Yes. She had ovarian cancer. Then two recurrences. The third bout was more than her body could bear."

"How awful."

They looked each other in the eyes in unspoken communication, a step toward knowing one another better that they both seemed to value.

"Do you have siblings?" she asked.

"No."

"Growing up, I spent most of my time alone with my travel fantasies."

"You spent a lot of time alone because you have no siblings, either?"

"That and my parents were away a lot." She'd already told him that they didn't have established careers.

"Who cared for you when they were gone?"

"No one."

"What do you mean?"

"They left me alone for weeks on end while they worked temporary jobs in other cities or states. Until I was eighteen when they left altogether." There she went again, telling him more than she'd ever told anybody. "Then I had to let the bank foreclose on the house because

I couldn't pay the mortgage and they stopped sending money." Now she'd said even that out loud. It was part of the story, anyway. Actually, it was a great purge to say it to a total stranger who'd be out of her life shortly.

"Gracie, my goodness. How old were you when they started leaving you alone?"

"About twelve."

"Twelve! Did they have personal issues? Alcoholism or substance abuse?"

"No. They were just drifters who had no business having a child. So sometimes they pretended they didn't." She touched her stomach and then removed her hand quickly. *Must stop that habit.* That was a different matter entirely. *Old news.*

"How did you manage at that age? What did you do?"

"I went to school. Back then they'd send money every so often for groceries or bills. I earned extra money shoveling snow from people's driveways."

"Yet after such a troubling childhood, you have such a pleasant disposition. Not everyone would."

She smiled, having never thought of it that way. Forward thinking was indeed her strong suit. Maybe, in her mind only, to show her parents and the Davis types of the world that she was worth caring about. Of course, it didn't matter because she'd never let herself rely on anyone ever again. "That's nice of you to say. A few other things dragged me down but now I feel like I'm on my way." She didn't need to tell him *everything*.

"I'm moved by your self-reliance."

"Oh, yes. I only count on myself. I'll be flying solo for the rest of my life."

"Here's to you, Gracie," he said as he lifted his wineglass for another toast. She clinked it with his and took a sip that tasted like validation. No one had ever analyzed her in such terms. What would it be like to be with a man who respected her, who she trusted? She'd never know. It was essential to always remember the words she'd just uttered. That she'd never get close to anyone again. Never let anyone take pieces of her heart away. She didn't have anything left to spare.

Why did she feel so comfortable talking to Ras? After Davis she was steering clear of men and, most certainly, of men from a totally different station in life, which would always be an issue. Yet Ras didn't act superior to her, even with his obvious status. She felt heard around him. It was a feeling she'd never had before.

He made her think of desires she didn't allow herself. Or maybe it was that she'd never met anyone who stirred up yearning in her like he did. She could imagine moving past talking with their words. That they could communicate in a different, nonverbal language. Learn more about each other through their bodies, through bringing each other appreciation and pleasure. She bit her lip. None of that was going to happen. Even if he wanted to do that, Gracie wouldn't take the risk of starting to care about him. And she didn't know a thing about chance encounters.

They went quiet for a minute. Both of them gazing out to the distance of the dining room. Gracie noticed families. Beautiful young children were on their best behavior as parents cut up food on their plates. Older kids whispered among themselves. Other tables were filled with fours and sixes, perhaps friends who regularly cruised together. Many more tables were occupied by couples. Casual dressers in outdoorsy clothes, perhaps just grabbing a bite after an afternoon of sport. Older couples for whom just enjoying the vistas from the ship made for a lovely vacation.

Then there were the lovers, the honeymooners, the anniversary celebrants. Gracie especially liked to watch the couples who were madly in love. The way the world around them disappeared and all that existed was each other. That would never be her. But it touched her heart nonetheless.

"You wouldn't by chance want to…?" Ras leaned closer and then stopped himself. "No, of course not."

After dinner, Ras walked Gracie to her stateroom. What serendipity it had been that she'd chosen the same restaurant as he had. Truth be told, he'd felt awkward sitting alone. A group of young women had failed at subtlety as they'd obviously gestured toward him, giggling and trying to catch his eye. One even passed by his table presumably on her way to the ladies' room, sauntering slowly in hopes of engaging his interest. Then there was his own caution that he was being followed, although there was no evidence of that. Anybody could recognize him as royalty and snap photos on their phone. On top of it was always the possibility that real paparazzi were around, ready to pounce on a juicy story about the prince on a cruise ship. Ras had hoped to leave his cares behind for his weeks on this journey. Which he seemed to be able to do when Gracie was by his side. So, he was glad she was back. Of course, it helped that he hadn't told her who he was.

"What are you doing tomorrow?" he asked as they strolled, making conversation as well as asking just out of curiosity.

"In the afternoon there is that industry group tour. We'll see the kitchens, the spa, the pool areas, different stateroom configurations. Then we have a tasting menu dinner in one of the private dining rooms."

"That sounds wonderful."

"What will *you* do?"

"I haven't decided yet."

He'd triple-checked that his private yacht was ready for him to leave *Liberation* the day after to board his true vessel for his trip. Due to the private nature of his venture, he'd booked the details of the yacht himself rather than have his personal secretary do so. Given the advantage that money was no object, in fact his mother had set aside a fund in hopes that Ras would make this journey, he'd requested the best of everything. An enormous yacht would await him, far larger than what he needed but one in which he could be comfortable to breathe deeply, sleep soundly and amuse himself however he wanted to. Something he hadn't done since his mother died.

"So what will you do in Miami the day after tomorrow?" he asked, knowing this might really be the last he'd see of her. Speaking of enjoying himself, admiring the caramel glisten in Gracie's eyes and the undulating waves of her hair were quite pleasant pursuits.

"I'll do a bus tour of the city and view the famous South Beach hotels. Then a seafood dinner. Then a visit to one of the Cuban nightclubs for dancing. What about you?"

Hmm, he didn't want to explain that he'd be doing none of that because he would leave *Liberation* and head straight to his yacht. But now that he thought about it, why not see the sights of Miami, having never been there before? He could change his plans, couldn't he? Wasn't spontaneity supposed to be part of this escape? What if he tagged along with Gracie, who seemed to know what was worth seeing, and then left after that? How would he explain it to her, though, when he didn't get back on the cruise at the end of the evening?

"Is that a preorganized itinerary that the cruise line offers? On a bus?"

"Yes. It sounds like cruise excursions are unfamiliar to you?"

He couldn't tell her that was because royalty wouldn't travel on a bus with the general public. Which didn't sound like a good idea. Close-up with a group of other passengers for a long period of time? Too much opportunity for someone to recognize him.

"I'm curious. What other excursions are offered?"

"On a typical cruise there would be dozens. But given this is such a short one, there were only a few. There were water sports. And one to explore the neighborhoods and Miami's ethnic food markets. I chose the bus because in one day it gives an overview of the city."

As they continued toward her stateroom, he thought to himself. What if he hired a car with a personal tour guide who could show him and Gracie all of those sights privately? He'd still have to figure out how to end the night and get Gracie back on the boat without him. Ah! If he wasn't heading straight to the yacht, he wouldn't have his luggage with him. They'd return at the end of the night to their respective staterooms. Then he'd get his bags and leave the ship a second time, Gracie tucked away in her bed by then.

The idea of spending the day with her in Miami filled him with elation. Yet maybe it was both unwise and unfair to steal her away, without telling her who he really was. Although it would be just half a day. It wasn't as if he was going to break her heart. Nor she break his. Hmm, strangely he wasn't so sure about that. He needed to think this out. When they reached the door to her stateroom, he held his tongue from saying anything further. Or tried to.

What slipped right out was, "Thank you for a lovely dinner. Will you have breakfast with me in the morning?" This was supposed to be his personal endeavor yet all he wanted to do was experience everything with Gracie. Harmless diversion, he figured. Besides, they'd for sure be apart the rest of the day after breakfast because she had her tour and tasting dinner. That would create some forced time away and he could settle down. It was just so nice to have her company. To hear the eagerness in her voice as she talked about her career ambitions after the unfathomable obstacles that she'd had to overcome. She was feminine and warm-blooded, which charged into his own masculinity.

"I have to warn you," Gracie said with a smile, "I've already read about the pancake sampler in the morning and I'm definitely going. They're offering ten kinds of pancakes with twenty different toppings. I intend to eat myself senseless."

Ras chuckled and then Gracie did too, and he was sure he could actually see the sizzle that flew through the air between them. "What time shall I come for you?"

"Ten."

"Until then." He caught himself leaning toward her, halfway to giving her a kiss on the cheek. Thankfully, he righted himself and instead bowed his shoulders to her. She swiped her key card and slipped into her room. When he heard the click locking her in, he figured he'd better go back to his stateroom as the Carat crew probably wouldn't look too favorably on him standing in front of Gracie's room all night. Tempting as it was.

Once in his own suite, he toed off his shoes and took off the new jacket that had felt quite comfortable for dinner indoors with its lightweight fabric. What an interesting dinner it had been. Gracie's knowledge of the East Coast was a stroke of luck. While he'd planned to roam at will, she'd given him some marvelous suggestions. It almost felt like they were mapping the trip together, which was, of course, ridiculous. He was engaged to be married and Princess Vajhana had already picked out a destination for their honeymoon, a particular Greek island. As he recalled her exact words were, "Everyone there is a *somebody*." In time he'd resume some circumspect meetups with women, but he'd play the husband game at first for the sake of appearances.

He sat down on the sofa and, uncharacteristically, put his feet up on the coffee table. Which brought a smile to his face as it was something any man might do but His Royal Highness Prince Rasmayada wouldn't. In the complete privacy of his stateroom, not a valet or assistant in sight, there was no harm in it.

He reflected over and over again on Gracie's shocking confessions about her childhood. What kind of people would leave a child of twelve years old to fend for herself for long periods of time? Not only was it immoral, it must have been illegal. And while she said it took her a number of years, and apparently some other hardships, to move into the career she wanted, she was doing it. Her grit and bravery were even more beautiful than her face. If that was possible. He hoped for the best for her from here on in. She deserved it. There was something so authentic about her, he'd found himself talking about his mother, something he hadn't done in a long time.

In contrast, he had a call to make.

"Where *are* you?" Vajhana's voice sounded

irritated. Ras could hear the voices of other people in the background. In fact, it sounded like a party.

"I'm still in the States. Where are *you*?"

"Paris. I absolutely had to shop for clothes, and you know there's not a thing to be had on our islands."

"Princess," a deep voice called out to her, which Ras heard. "Look what I have for you." Vajhana laughed in that over-the-top dramatic way she had.

"Who's that?" Ras asked.

"No one you know."

"When are you going home? I'll be there in a couple of weeks."

"I will, too. I've got photographers coming from Singapore and Milan to do features on us, we still haven't finalized the seating arrangements and surely you don't expect me to go to that boring fundraiser for the Marine Biology Foundation alone."

No, certainly Vajhana wouldn't want to attend a function simply because her name might help that charity attract important donors. Sometimes Ras thought Vajhana had no idea what it meant to be a princess. That it wasn't about jewels and shoes and not having to wait in line to get into a club. Furthermore, someday she would also be queen to his king just as her older brother would sit on her island's throne someday. What Ras wanted in her was a wife and partner, someone who would set an example in kindness and rationale, someone who wouldn't take anything for granted. Of course, what he longed for was a woman like the greatest queen the island had ever known. His mother.

In Vajhana, he'd have to accept a different kind of queen. Their fathers had made the decision to unite for the betterment of their subjects. Although Ras still questioned whether caring for the land was just as much an obligation as caring for its people. He didn't like the proposals for the massive manufacturing plants they were developing with the Thai conglomerate PTG corporation.

"Oh, Princess," that male voice Ras heard through the phone cajoled. Could it be what it sounded like it was? That Vajhana wasn't even exercising the most basic courtesy of discretion in her liaisons? Ras ended the call. Annoyance began to dot his forehead. He texted a mutual friend who he knew could find out the truth about what was really going on.

"Your pancake escort has arrived, madam," Ras said with an outstretched hand when Gracie opened her stateroom door. She wore another one of her adorable flower-patterned dresses, this one white with big yellow roses. It flared out at the knees, and along with the ballet-type shoes, she looked like a New Yorker in the 1950s, hurrying through the busy streets. No wonder she was able to help him pick out clothes yesterday; she had her own personal style. With her friendly face, he supposed she'd look good in anything. After his distasteful conversation with Vajhana last night, he was in the mood for Gracie's freshness. He wasn't even sure how he'd make it through the day without her. Which was probably a sign that he needed to, to let his growing heat for her cool off. She was not a woman to have a dalliance with. He sensed that with her, it wouldn't be so easy to have a passing fancy.

"Good because I'm famished," she said, greeting him with zeal. "It took all I had to resist the snacks in the room's basket. I did have a cup of tea already."

"Pancake emergency, then. Let's go." He wanted to match her vivacity. All of His Royal Highness's moves were usually scheduled and measured, which was how it should be. Yet he felt like taking her by the hand so they could run through the ship in pursuit of their treats.

Thankfully, decorum told him to simply gesture toward the corridor. He followed right behind her as they made their way to a sunny breakfast room constructed mostly of glass. It was packed with passengers, reminding Ras, in case he'd forgotten who he was, that royalty was never to be in large crowds without accompaniment. He knew the reasons were for his safety. But surely a quick breakfast didn't present grave danger. His alarm reinforced the idea he was about to spring on Gracie.

"I'll have a ricotta lemon pancake, a pumpkin pecan, a banana coconut and a mixed berry." Gracie quickly rattled off the menu items with conviction when the server took her order.

Ras could only throw up his palms in surrender and say, "Same." Which gave all three of them a giggle.

"Does anyone *not* eat too much on a cruise?"

"Not knowing firsthand," he offered, "it's definitely a pleasure to try new foods. That Café Cubano yesterday afternoon was quite memorable. I typically take coffee with only milk. The Cubano was rich and sweet, but the bitterness kept it from being sugary. What shall we eat in Miami?"

"We?" She tilted her head at him in question.

Last night, he'd felt it was too much to bring up his idea, so he'd only asked her to breakfast.

"I'd like to make a suggestion." He'd been weighing his larger idea ever since it occurred to him. This new brainstorm would be a way to try out a short version, and if it didn't feel right, he wouldn't take it any further.

"What's that?" She licked a drop of pancake syrup from a corner of her mouth. He hoped she'd do it again.

"Rather than following the exact itinerary of that bus tour tomorrow, possibly having to stay too long or leave too soon at any of the destinations, I've reserved a private car to drive me around Miami. Would you join me?" He realized that was an odd proposal coming from someone she'd just met yesterday. He wished he could assure her that his intentions were respectable. Because he'd only be with her for a short time before he boarded his yacht never to see her again, he thought it best to persist in not revealing his identity. "As a travel agent, I'm sure you know the sights. In fact, can I hire you as my tour guide? I'll pay you for the day."

"Pay me?" she sputtered while taking a sip of orange juice.

"Why not? I'm not a murderer or a kidnapper, I promise you. I'm simply asking you to per-

form a service just as I'll be paying for a driver."
He gave her a figure that was double what he
was quoted to hire the driver. The fact that her
eyes went quite round told him that the number had gotten her attention. "Plus, don't you
think it would be more fun to tool around on our
own?" Not to mention keep him out of crowds.

While he couldn't read her mind, Ras sensed
she was considering the proposition, with skep-
ticism. He understood the reluctance to trust
strangers; after all, he was held apart from
them. Verbal assurance that he wasn't a murderer or a kidnapper was the best he could do.
She'd have to take a leap of faith.

"We'd spend the day and evening doing
whatever we want in Miami?"

"Exactly."

She forked into her pancakes for a few more
bites, contemplating his idea. "Okay. I'll do it
on one condition. That I choose all our destinations. I want to be able to make recommendations to future clients as to the best of Miami.
We can't see everything in a day, but we'll do
our best."

"Deal. I'll put myself in your hands." A rush
of oxygen whooshed through him at his own
words.

Might she have felt it too, as evidenced by the

peachy blush that came to her cheeks? There was nothing wrong with a little bit of harmless flirting was there? Other than the fact that he was soon to be married, the thought of which brought a snarl to his lips. How could he marry a woman he didn't love and who clearly didn't love him? He knew he needed to fulfill his duties to his homeland, but it was such a price to pay. His mother never would have approved of that, regardless of the impending partnership in industry. Ras knew she would say that nothing was more important than love. And she would have gotten the king to agree. They'd had a love story for the ages, after all. A gleam in the eye every time they saw each other. Secret signals and code words they had while in public and genuine smiles behind closed doors. Was Ras selfish for wanting that for himself? King Maho was very certain in his matchmaking of his son during his discussions with Princess Vajhana's father. In fact, he'd called for a meeting and made the motion himself. As Ras turned thirty, his father had made a unilateral decision about his son's matrimonial status.

Something ached in Ras's chest as he watched Gracie sip her coffee. It was a sad finality that he'd never be in love. Why did he have such a haunting, aching feeling that love was around him, like an aura that he could reach out for but never grab hold of?

Not able to take his eyes off Gracie's lovely face, a stunning insight blazed like a wildfire through him. While his father had signed deeds and contracts that the union between Ras and Vajhana was to benefit their nations' livelihoods, that wasn't the only reason for the arranged marriage. The king knew that Ras didn't love the princess. That was precisely why he thought Ras should marry her. He'd concocted this whole strategy to shield Ras from future pain. What if Ras was in love with the woman he married and she was taken from him? As the king's wife was. He didn't want his son to suffer that awful anguish and loss, the kind the king had never recovered from. He knew Ras would *never*, *ever* love Vajhana. In marrying him off to a woman he felt nothing for, the king was protecting his son, eliminating risk. Ras shook his head in the realization that his father was still a romantic after all.

CHAPTER FOUR

THE NEXT DAY as they walked down the gangway to disembark in Miami, Gracie tried not to let her excitement be too externally obvious. As a travel professional, she should be a bit more blasé. The truth was she'd never been to Miami and was thrilled to be there. She'd done her due diligence and taken virtual tours of all the hotels and major attractions, talked to other travel agents to get recommendations, and followed websites and social media accounts that had their pulse on what was new and cutting edge, where the latest sounds and tastes were. Nonetheless, she was looking forward to seeing everything in person. It was a bonus that *Liberation* was docking in this famous Florida city and that she'd have a chance to get to know it personally.

"There's our car." Ras pointed to the black sedan after he'd been texted the license plate identification. No driver holding up a tacky sign that read Ras. It occurred to Gracie that she still didn't know the last name of the man she was about to get into a car with. She didn't have a good track record on judging people. She fell for Davis, and he turned out to be rich in dollars but poor in character. He left her at a critical time, not wanting to take responsibility for what he helped create. Never knowing what transpired in his wake. Leaving Gracie with a double loss she'd never forget. She brushed her hand across her tummy.

She may not forgive or forget, but she was going to move forward. And apparently, in style today. Whoever Ras was, he was clearly used to the top-of-the-line in everything. She should have known he wasn't going to hire a compact car in a garish color. She wanted to sell luxury travel. Here it was.

"Great."

"Yes, please, come." He placed his hand on her elbow to help her onto the solid ground of Miami. Had he gotten over his original discomfort in touching her? Was it the breeze or his flat palm that swept over her, dredging up something that she'd stuffed deep down, a part of her that she'd been ignoring?

When they reached the car, the driver, in full

uniform and cap, opened the door for them to enter. Ras gestured for Gracie to get in first. Her hand slid across the butter-soft and plush black leather of the seat. The driver closed the door once Ras got in next to her. A strong virility emanated from his body.

There was no reason for them to be sitting right up against each other, the seat was long and wide enough to hold three people, yet there they were, neither of them making a move away. Ras reached into the beverage tray and pulled a frosty bottle of sparkling water from a bucket of ice. He cracked the cap and poured the fizz into two heavy crystal glasses.

"Let the driver know our first stop," Ras told her as he handed her a glass.

"South Beach. Please take us through Ocean Drive and Collins Avenue." She took a sip of the bubbly water.

In reference to the drink he said, "I assumed we'd have a cocktail later but that it was too early in the day now. Tell me about yesterday."

As they passed through the city streets, she gave him a description of the ship tour, saying that she was particularly impressed seeing the engine room and the inner workings of the vessel. She described a few of her favorite bites from the tasting menu dinner. What she left out was how much she'd missed him, how many times she'd thought of him. And that when she got back to her stateroom, how long the evening felt not having seen him. "How did you spend the day?"

"You might find this surprising, but I did something I haven't done in years. Ever maybe."

"What's that?"

"I laid in bed and watched movies."

She really wanted to ask him the big questions about himself. Where he was from, as the first time she'd asked he'd merely answered, *Asia*. She wondered what the family business he spoke of was that prevented him from spending a day in bed if he wanted to.

But she didn't need to know any of that and he wasn't offering to tell her, so what difference did it really make? She'd never see him again after the cruise. Although her skin felt tight at that notion. In a weird way she'd already become attached to him. She knew it was silly to get carried away with fairy tales, though. In reality, even if she clicked with Ras, she'd never get close to him because he'd desert her in the end. Her belief was supported with evidence.

The driver knew where to go. "Look at this architecture!" she exclaimed as they peeped out the window at the tall hotels. "These pastel-colored buildings make up the Art Deco Historic District."

"Fantastic," Ras agreed.

"Can you let us out here so we can take a walk?" she asked the driver, who pulled over.

Along the street, she pointed to this restaurant and that, at outdoor tables filled with people dressed in lightweight clothing. Palm trees were everywhere and the glistening beach, with seemingly thousands of people in the sand, was never out of sight.

"Was this whole area built at the same time?" he inquired.

"It was an evolution during the 1930s and '40s. Miami has always been a popular city to live or vacation in. For decades now, retirees from New York and surrounding areas move down here for the weather."

"I can see why. Shall we sit down at one of these establishments?"

"No, we're just here to walk. We'll eat in the Little Havana neighborhood."

"Okay. Whatever you say." He gave her a military salute, which made her chuckle.

After a lovely stroll, they got back in the car. "Calle Ocho," she told the driver. After the pastels of South Beach, Little Havana was an entirely different part of the city. Brightly colored paint adorned the buildings, murals and sculptures in the heart of the area. Gracie had the driver drop them off again, so that they could wander through the neighborhood on foot.

Even in the sunlight of day, Cuban music could be heard coming from businesses and street corners. "This is so vibrant and alive. I love the verve," Ras said after his customary inventory of everyone on the streets. He always seemed to worry that he was being observed. After he'd tried to shield her from looking at the magazines in the ship's gift shop, she'd gathered that he was in some way famous, maybe within whatever industry he was in. And he didn't want her to know, wanted their connection to remain anonymous. That was fine with her, although she couldn't resist being curious.

They walked through several of the streets, admiring the artwork in the many galleries. "Ras, here's the important question."

"Oh…okay," he said, expressing trepidation.

"What do you feel like eating?"

He grinned with relief. "What's traditional?"

"Perhaps *ropa vieja*." She didn't speak Spanish except when it came to food, and then she could make her way pretty well. "Believe it or not, that translates to *old clothes*."

"Doesn't sound very appetizing."

"It really doesn't. But it's delicious. Shredded meat in a sauce of onions and peppers."

"Yes. I want to try everything," he said, making eye contact that was so strangely penetrating it rattled through her.

Gracie felt happy, the happiest she had in as far back as she could remember. This was *her thing*. This was what she wanted. She was visiting a new place, throwing all of her senses into it. And, much to her surprise, it was all the better with this interesting man by her side.

Ras pushed the plate away from him when it was empty. "Well, I should be hungry again in three or four days."

Gracie smiled after swallowing a bite. The savory *ropa vieja* was balanced with its side dish of *arroz y frijoles negro*, rice and black beans. "Yes, it's very filling."

"Scrumptious, though." He wasn't in the habit of using words like *scrumptious*. He didn't usually get emotional about food or scenery. Yet this trip was different. On this trip he did.

"You are finished?" the waitress asked.

"Did I leave a drop?" he joked.

"I will tell the dishwasher he does not have to spend too much time on this plate."

"Is this a family business?" he asked her as Gracie observed the conversation.

"Yes, my mother is at the front today," she said while pointing to the woman who'd seated them. "My aunt and brothers run the kitchen. And my son helps wait on the tables at night." She cleared the plates and left their table. Chatting with people, without that built-in distance because they were commoners and he was a prince, was exactly what his mother had wanted him to experience. He even enjoyed the unfamiliarity of doing so.

"You mentioned that you were involved in a family business as well," Gracie commented.

"Yes, in fact we have an upcoming merger with another family." He was being purposely cryptic but he almost grimaced thinking about Vajhana, off in Paris doing heaven knew what. Checking his phone now and then, he awaited a report from his old friend Niran who would scope out what was really going on.

Ras and Vajhana both knew their marriage involved the economic future of two nations and had nothing to do with two hearts. Nonetheless, Ras expected at least decorum from her. If she was going to have extramarital liaisons, he'd hoped she'd pay great attention to keeping them away from their fathers, the staff at the palaces and the public. As he would. Laughter and shrieking on the other end of the phone hadn't garnered confidence in Ras that his fiancée was behaving herself circumspectly.

"You say that as if you don't approve of the partnership," Gracie noted. Ah, so he wasn't even hiding his displeasure well.

"My father and the other interested party," he explained, meaning Vajhana's father, King Yodfa of Ko Yaolum, "are planning to work with a manufacturing conglomerate on some islands they hold guardianship of. I'm against the idea because that type of industry will cause depletion to the area's natural resources." Of course he was referring to Ko Pha Lano as well, his home and the place where the island's long-term well-being would fall on his shoulders in later years. It would be then any damage due to the decisions made now would be felt. How would he explain it to his subjects, when the waters were contaminated and the land became unfarmable?

"Do you have an alternative plan?"

"I think cultivating environmentally friendly tourism would be better stewardship." Which could provide employment to the people of both islands and sustainability to the land and its resources. Both kings had rejected Ras's suggestion. "But that's not the direction my father and the other decision maker want to go in." It was hard to say which was more frustrating, the hardheaded, old-fashioned thinking of the two kings with regard to development or to arranged marriages.

"It sounds like you care quite a bit about the outcome."

"Hmm." Of course he did; he was the crown prince. His computer was filled with files of research about ecotourism and schematics, many specifically with regard to marine conservation.

"Coffee or dessert?" the waitress interrupted.

"No, thank you. Gracie?" She indicated no, and the waitress left the check on their table. Changing to a less heated topic, he asked, "Where are we going next?"

"Do you want to do something unusual?" she asked with a little snark as if it was a dare. She was very sexy. Very. Plain and simple. He wondered if she realized how alluring she was. And why some man hadn't already swept her off her feet and made her his.

"Unusual." He licked his lips. "You have me intrigued."

"Would you like to see the Florida Everglades?"

"Why not? Are they nearby?"

"They are. And we'll see them on an airboat. There are several tour companies. I can look them up and buy us tickets."

"You mean there are group airboats?"

"Yes."

"Let's book a private airboat. Just the two of us and the driver." He handed her his phone. "Make the arrangements and then I'll pay."

"Regardless of cost, I assume?" A minute later they were booked, and she handed him the phone back to authorize payment.

"We'll be more comfortable, if it's only you and I." He sat on those words for a minute. Feeling them inside.

"Everglades National Park, here we come."

As they were leaving the restaurant, the waitress yelled out, *"Gracias."*

"Adios," Gracie said back.

The driver brought them to the national park, and they walked a trail that led to a pond where there were many species of birds. Gracie gasped. "Oh, goodness, look at the blue coloring on that one."

"Is it a heron?"

"There's an app that can identify the bird if we load in a photo." She pulled out her phone and lifted her graceful arm to get a good shot.

With a few taps she quickly got the result. "Yep, a great blue heron. Common to wetlands areas."

They studied a flock of spoonbills.

"There's an egret," Ras said, pointing in a different direction.

"Wow, I don't think I've ever seen one of those before."

Ras loved this. One minute they were in the hipster South Beach, the next in the culturally rich Little Havana. And now in serene nature, reminding him that he didn't want to see the natural beauty of Ko Pha Lano disintegrate from decades of exposure to toxic industry.

"Gracie, you're doing a great job as a tour guide. I wish I could hire you to be my personal travel agent." There he went again, saying something that could be interpreted as flirty!

"Hold your praise until you see if you like the airboat."

When it was time for their ride, they arrived at the plank wood dock to be welcomed by a white-haired man with a matching beard who introduced himself as Captain Clyde. He handed each of them a pair of headphones. "Welcome aboard. You'll be wanting these as the boat is loud, and they also let you talk to each other and hear me babble." They both grinned as they took their seats. "Have you ever been on an airboat?"

Both Ras and Gracie shook their heads no.

"Basically, it's a flat-bottomed boat that uses an aircraft-type propeller." Captain Clyde pointed behind him at the giant propeller wheel in its cage. "You'll want to refrain from letting your arms or legs get near the propeller if you'd like to take them home with you."

As they started away from the shore the sound was, indeed, deafening, and they immediately put their headphones on.

"The Everglades National Park is home to dozens upon dozens of species of wildlife." The captain's voice came in through the headset as they skimmed across the water. "That includes over two hundred thousand alligators. We might get lucky and see a crocodile or two as well, this being one of the only places in the world where the two coexist."

They traveled through mangrove tunnels, the parts of the water where the coastal trees didn't grow. Birds flew up above, and the wind blew in their faces. Ras felt far away from everything, in a magical world that didn't belong to humans. So when his phone buzzed and he glanced down to see it was Niran, he stuffed the device back into his pocket. The news about Vajhana's escapades could wait.

The captain directed them to notice a family of raccoons, climbing through and among dry twigs above the water. The black masks around their eyes made them distinct from every other animal Ras could think of. He knew that even though they looked cuddly, they weren't. Nonetheless, they were magnificent to watch.

Gracie studied the baby kits, three of them, as they frolicked around their mother. Her smile was so celestial there were almost tears in her eyes. Ras reached over and put his hand atop hers, immediately reacting to how tender her skin was. Funny, but touching her had become the most natural thing in the world to him. She turned to give him a half smile, which covered him like a ray of sun peeking through the thick sawgrass of the marshes.

Captain Clyde's voice continued in their ears as he gestured to a huge, scaly sunbather. "We've spotted ourselves a crocodile. Do you folks know how to tell the difference between a crocodile and an alligator?" They both shook their heads. "You can tell by their snouts. The croc's is long and pointy whereas the gator's is shorter and rounded."

The crocodile, asleep with his mouth wide

open, looked ominous, but the captain told them that was normal. Then, from under water beside the boat, an alligator popped its head above the surface, startling them. Another sprang up on the other side of the boat. Gracie's eyes opened wide.

"Now, you folks don't want to be getting too close to the gators. Although they don't eat humans," Captain Clyde explained reassuringly. "Not so far, anyway."

Without question, theirs was the only chauffeured car driving out of Everglades National Park. That was sightseeing, Ras style. The driver pulled onto the highway returning to Miami. They'd had a wonderful time on the airboat marveling at all the wildlife they saw. Now they were headed for an evening at Club de Magia, which translated to Magic Club, one of the city's biggest Cuban nightspots. After that, they'd reboard *Liberation* and sleep while it looped northward, making its way back to New York.

"Captain Clyde was quite a character," Ras chuckled. "Especially when he told you that the alligators…"

"That's gators, to the locals," Gracie corrected him.

"When he told you that particular big daddy we saw had a penchant for blond hair."

She scrunched up her mouth. "Yeah, he had me for a minute there."

"I couldn't blame the gator if it was true, though." With a tilt of the head, she studied him. "Why are you looking at me like that?"

"I'm not used to receiving compliments," she said. Everywhere they'd been, money and luxury were no object. He still hadn't said specifically what he did for a living but had spoken of stewardship of land. Not that it mattered any to her, yet she was still bemused that the man who'd hired a private tour guide and driver was also so nice to the waitress serving him *ropa vieja* at an informal lunch.

"You should be, Gracie. Is it too personal of me to ask if you've been in a relationship?"

"I never will be again."

"Oh, that's right, the wanderer with her online travel agency."

"Right."

"After you've fulfilled your dream, could you see yourself settling down? Having children?"

She looked past him out the window as the car sped through the miles. When she concentrated hard enough, she'd learned how to swallow back the tears. All of them. *Do not put your hand on your stomach.* "I wouldn't know anything about having children. I told you, my parents didn't exactly set any kind of example." The truth was, she adored children. Certainly she'd spent time contemplating whether having her own, loving and caring for them, would be the best revenge for everything she'd missed out on. That's why she'd been so happy at first when it looked like all the pieces were going to fit with Davis. What a disaster that was. And now, even though she'd never get into a relationship again, there was always the possibility of having children alone. She did think about that. A lot.

"I think you'd be a terrific mother."

"I was in a long-term relationship once. His name was Davis."

"What happened?"

"He left me."

"Why?"

"After the way my parents were always off doing whatever they wanted, I was desperate for someone who would stick around. I met Davis and moved from Trenton to a beach house in Point Pleasant his grandmother left him when she died."

"That sounds like a promising start."

"You would assume so. But he was out all

the time, not bringing me along. He was very controlling, wanted me to live with him and be faithful even though he was never around."

"That's odd."

"Not really. He was from a wealthy family and I was born on the wrong side of the tracks. I was good enough to be kept at home but not to be seen out with."

"Oh. I see."

She wished Ras would have sounded more indignant but with his mergers and islands, he probably only dated the *right kind* of girls, too.

"I was so relieved to have a steady job and a place to live, not having to panic if a check from my parents didn't arrive like I used to, that I went along with it. And then…" She stopped herself. She hated this part of the story and so she didn't have to tell it. She barely knew Ras. He didn't need all the details. He was clearly keeping some secrets of his own.

Do not put your hand on your stomach.

"Anyway, it just didn't work out."

By the time they got back to the city, it was nighttime and the clubs were beginning to fill up. Gracie had chosen Club de Magia because it was one of the most renowned, and they featured live music all night. They walked into the sounds of a horn section and Latin percussion.

The club was massive. The inner circle held the stage and an enormous dance floor. The next level was filled with tall cocktail tables and barstools. And the top level was for tables and booths. "Shall I get us a booth?" Ras asked. She nodded and he approached the hostess, a stunning woman in a tight orange dress and bright lipstick.

They were shown to a half-circle-shaped booth in the center of the top tier. Ras had probably arranged it because it was so big and tall that it was quite private. The seat was upholstered in a deep purple velvet. Before they were asked, a server came over with two drinks on a tray. "*Buenos noches.* Can I offer you a mojito?"

"Ooh, yes, those look fabulous," Gracie answered quickly. The waiter placed down two coasters with the club's logo of a top hat and rabbit, homage to the traditional magician's trick. He placed the drinks on top, frosty highball glasses with big sprigs of mint.

She lifted hers to toast with Ras. "To adventure. From Art Deco to *ropa vieja* to gators to salsa," he said with a clink of his. "You've shown me a day I'll never forget."

"To adventure. The night is still young." They sipped.

"Oh, my gosh, that is the best thing I've ever tasted."

"Simple perfection. Rum, sugar, sparkling water, lime and mint."

"It's been many hours since we've eaten. What shall we have?"

"Do you feel like a sandwich? I want you to taste the classic Cubano."

"Whatever it is, I'm in," he said with a laugh. "I'm so glad I decided to hire you, Gracie. You're not like most of the women I know." His smile quickly faded like it had just dawned on him that he'd forgotten something.

"Is something wrong?"

He took a long pause to consider the question. "Absolutely not."

The waiter approached and Ras gestured to her to order. "Two Cubanos."

The band launched into a fiery rhythm that prompted many people to make their way from the tables to the dance floor. "What do you think? Shall we?" he suggested.

"I'm game if you are."

Ras stood up and reached his hand down to take hers. Gracie didn't know what it was, but between the music, the gentle clasp of her hand and his sincere smile, she felt like she was leading someone else's life. Thoughts she hadn't had in years kept popping up. What it might be like to truly *be* with someone. To share life. Weather the ups and downs. Create a union together that was bigger than the sum of its parts. That meant something. That meant everything.

No, Gracie reminded herself. It was fine to play pretend for a couple of hours in a city where they were nameless tourists. In reality, she'd never put her heart on the line again. She'd charted her course, and she was going to stick to it.

Even if Ras's eyes made her speculate beyond anything she'd ever dared before.

Once they got to the dance floor, the beats drummed into her body and she started to sway. Ras faced her as they found the tempo. "Do you know how to salsa?" she asked him, making an assumption that he might be more the waltz type. Yet he surprised her by taking the lead with the basic left, right, together, right, left, together steps. Within a few bars, they got into a groove. She placed her hand on one of his muscular shoulders. The flat of his large palm against her back made her eyelashes flutter.

Gracie felt the sexiest she ever had. Was it her imagination or was it in the way Ras looked at her? Goodness, even though she'd only known him for a hot minute, it was going to be hard to say goodbye when this wild ride ended. Would that be tonight when they returned to the ship? Or would they spend the rest of the time until they returned to New York together? Her convictions about staying away from men were fraying at the seams when she was with him.

After a few songs, the band segued to a slower rhythm. The couples on the dance floor brought each other to a close embrace. Gracie took an immediate step backward, figuring Ras wasn't going to want to dance as lovers do, and wasn't going to pull her close. She thought she'd save them from awkwardness.

However, she apparently had it wrong because as she started to move away, he wrapped his long arm around her waist, encircling her in a way that made her core melt. His other hand took hers and brought it to his collarbone. She was almost woozy as they began to sway, quickly finding their flow. His body melded into hers until she could feel every bone underneath his skin. And no matter how wide she swung, that firm anchor of his arm brought her back over and over. To him. *To him.*

After the trance they reached, he eventually snapped back to survey the crowd in the dim lighting of the club, perhaps reaching his limit of the sensual dancing, ending the moment and providing both of them with relief. "We'd better return to the table before our Cubanos get cold," he suggested. Leading her by the hand, they slid back into the booth and had a sip of their refreshing mojitos. The sandwiches did arrive shortly after. Ras took a bite and then rolled his eyes in a comic way that made her laugh. "Why do you keep feeding me one delectable thing after the other? What alchemy is in this deliciousness?"

"It's ham, roast pork, cheese, pickles, mustard and bread placed into a sandwich press so that the center gets gooey and the bread becomes crusty. Another very simple combination that yields a yummy result."

They chatted about travel. On the West Coast of the US, he loved Seattle and San Francisco. He started to say something else, then scrapped the idea. A minute later it returned.

"Let me share something with you," he began. "I'm not returning to New York on *Liberation*."

That was strange.

"Oh, is everything okay?"

"Yes. This has always been my plan. I've got

a private yacht waiting at the Miami harbor. As I told you, I'm going to tour the East Coast."

"By yacht?"

"Yes. That way I can go wherever I want and decide how long I want to stay. Just as we've done today rather than in a group."

"Why did you board *Liberation* in the first place?"

"I'm recognizable, so I wanted to throw any possible followers off my track. I figured no one would expect me to be on a short public cruise."

"You're not sleeping on *Liberation* tonight?" In spite of herself, she felt a little disappointed. She, too, had a spectacular day today. In fact, the most fun she'd had in ages.

"Gracie, I have a proposition for you. Just as we've done today, I'd like to offer you a job as my tour guide. For the time that I'll be here. I'll be much less noticeable if I'm traveling with a woman, as if we were just an ordinary couple. Plus I'd love for you to show me all of the great spots."

"A personal tour guide?"

"Yes. You name your price."

"I'd stay with you on your private yacht?" While Ras had been nothing but a perfect gentleman, Gracie found his offer more than a little unusual. "And this would be just as your guide and traveling companion?" She didn't want to insinuate that he'd be less than honorable, but this was not a typical offer.

"Of course. You'll have your own suite onboard. The yacht I've chartered is lavish. Top-of-the-line, with a pool, a cinema, a spa, deluxe bathrooms, three dining rooms."

Her first impulse was to say no. She'd only just met him, and he obviously had some skeletons in the closet. No one in their right mind would take off on a yacht with a stranger. Even one whose touch made her breath sputter. To whom she'd opened up about some of her own past, details that she'd never told anyone. A man who made her feel desirable and indispensable. Even still, this couldn't be a wise idea.

"Ras, I don't even know your full name, where you're from, what you actually do for a living. I'm sure you can understand that it seems less than prudent for me to go sailing away on your yacht."

He smiled wistfully, as if he'd just contemplated the proposition from *her* perspective. "Of course. I'm sorry that I'm not able to share the details of my identity. I can assure you, though, that the yacht crew will be on board with us at all times. And I give you my word that your safety, comfort and protection will be at the forefront of our journey."

It was a hunch that could prove disastrous, yet her gut told her his words were true, that he'd make sure no harm fell on her.

"I'd have total control over our destinations and sights?"

"Why yes, that would be the point. Wouldn't that benefit your travel career?"

Yes, it would. She'd never be able to afford to travel in the style Ras did. Top shelf, money no object. It was a chance to see things she'd never seen through a once-in-a-lifetime lens. Afterward, she'd be able to speak with first-hand knowledge about deluxe experiences on the East Coast.

What difference did it make that Ras was a mystery? This was just a business opportunity.

"So, what, we'd go back to the ship to get our bags and then disembark again?"

CHAPTER FIVE

RAS HAD WAITED long enough. He'd been having such a beautiful evening with Gracie, he didn't want to let real life interrupt. Especially when they'd danced with their bodies so close and in sync to the Latin beats, both of them losing themselves in the loud music and in each other's rhythms. The club was dark enough that his concern about being spotted was abated. How they'd organically moved through the salsa, and the rhumba and, especially the ballads. Like they'd been dancing together for ages, anticipating each other, welcoming each other. And the smell of her perfume had sent a surge through him. He could still inhale a whiff of it next to him in the car as it took them back to the cruise ship to pack up.

But now it was time to truly face the music. He needed to read the text his friend Niran had left him about Vajhana, what she was doing in

Paris and with whom. He held his phone toward him, already suspecting, no, knowing, in his heart what Niran's messages were going to be.

He wasn't wrong.

Didn't realize this was news, sorry to be the bearer. Vajhana is in flagrant cahoots with a British earl named Cyril. Sources saw them checking into various Parisian hotels. Her Royal Highness was photographed sitting on the earl's lap while they smooched at a club. They're inseparable, traipsing in and out of shops on the Champs-Élysées. Again, assumed you knew. He's not the first.

Ras's jaw clenched, and he could almost hear the ticking where the bones met his ears. His breath became very fast and his hands turned to tight fists. In fact, all of the muscles in his body tightened as he leaned deliberately back against the seat. The sheer shamelessness of her behavior made him see red, even if it wasn't a surprise.

"Is something wrong?" Gracie sensed the changes in his body language.

"An unfortunate report on the business proposal I was telling you about."

"I'm sorry to hear that." The kindness in

her voice reached his subconscious. With deep breaths, his oxygen intake gradually slowed. His mouth relaxed, releasing the gritting of his teeth. After the sting of the confirmation subsided, he realized that he felt nothing. It was humiliating that she was behaving so indiscreetly, but it was just information. They were going to need to come to better terms than these if they were going to have an enduring partnership.

When they boarded *Liberation*, he and Gracie parted to pack up their belongings, agreeing to meet back at the same spot in twenty minutes. The tiniest curve of his lip told him just how glad he was that she had agreed to travel with him. She was a delightful companion. He genuinely enjoyed every moment he'd spent with her. Her gusto for all the sights and sounds and tastes they'd experienced was contagious. With her, he felt that freedom that he'd set out to find. And honest conversation flowed between them. Well, honesty on her part. On his personal identity, not so much. She didn't know that he was a prince, let alone an engaged one. Nonetheless, this chance partnership was exactly what he needed. Now more than ever.

There was nothing wrong in spending time with a woman he met on this trip. But he did make a mental promise to himself that even though he was physically attracted to her, he would not let anything happen between them. Gracie was off-limits. She didn't deserve to be treated as a secretive, short-term fling. Which she wasn't at all. He knew she'd been hurt by parents who didn't meet her needs and by a boyfriend who'd treated her badly. He wasn't going to add to her list. He did have a moment's lament after hearing about Vajhana's carelessness, a wish that he was set to marry a woman he loved and who loved him, like his mother would have wanted. A woman like…

It took a mere few minutes to pack up the small case he'd brought along from New York and the new bag he'd bought on ship for his purchases from the menswear shop. His Royal Highness was still quite unused to carrying his own luggage. A simple act he quite liked. Once he joined Gracie at the meeting spot, with a tug he took her bag, too.

"Ready?" he asked.

"Ready."

As they left *Liberation*, he informed the attendant that they wouldn't be returning to the ship. Soon he, the bags and Gracie were back onto Florida ground. A limo was waiting. This time, it was to take them to the harbor. They were headed even further away from reality.

* * *

When the yacht's captain reached for Gracie's hand to help her step aboard *Destiny*, she couldn't believe her eyes. While she'd studied private yachts online and had even gone to look at them at local harbors, nothing had prepared her for the grandeur and size of the vessel Ras had reserved.

"My gosh, this is spectacular!" she exclaimed, taking in its sparkling clean hull and polished brass railings.

"Welcome to your home away from home. I hope you'll be comfortable."

"Good evening. I am Captain Ernesto. May I introduce you to the crew?" The captain was a trim man with short gray hair and a short beard, who wore a traditional uniform. "This is David and this is Neo," he said, pointing to the two men, both in crisp khaki shorts and white polo shirts.

"Hello."

"It's our pleasure to serve you in every possible way so do let us know how we can best accomplish that."

"Thank you."

"If you'd like, I can show you around the ship and then perhaps you'd like to settle in for the night. We'll set off in the morning. Can we bring you a late supper or some snacks?"

Ras looked at her to decide. Even though they'd had those delightful Cubano sandwiches, after all their dancing, she wouldn't mind a little bite before bed. "Gracie?"

"Some snacks and a cup of herbal tea would be nice, thank you."

"If you'll follow me, then," the captain said, "let me show you the cabins."

They went up the stairs to the top deck. When they stepped inside, it was beyond Gracie's imagination. The entire deck, from bow to stern, was devoted to one master bedroom suite. The perimeter was lined with 360 degrees of shaded glass panels so that guests could see out in any direction but no one could see in. The whole deck was one room! Gracie didn't even know such a thing existed.

Within the area, a salon had contemporary sofas and chaise lounges, all done in earthy colors. Side tables were placed here and there with a huge display of pink flowers on the coffee table. Nearby was a bar area, its own private pub with shelves of liquor, beers, wine and soft drinks of every conceivable variety. A half dozen bar tools were arranged on a stand at the ready.

Sliding glass doors opened out to a wooden balcony. At that late hour, both the water and the moon glistened. They stepped out while the captain adjusted the night lighting so they could see. A row of lounge chairs with stuffed cushions surrounded a lap pool. There was a section for entertaining as well, a big wrap-around sofa with white and red cushions that created a separate space. Yet a different part of the balcony had a dining table set with chairs for eight. In another nook was a king-size bed strewn with dozens of decorative pillows, a canopy, and curtains for privacy. An outdoor bed. For lazy naps breathing in the sea air. And… Her mind thought all sorts of things that it shouldn't.

Captain Emilio briefly showed them some of the convenience systems. Various areas of the outdoor deck had remote-controlled awnings to allow as little or as much direct sun as they wanted. "Of course, please ring for a crew member to assist you with anything."

It was probably past midnight after their long day of sightseeing, Miami's neighborhoods and the Everglades tour, finishing up with the dancing. A shiver ran through her as she replayed key moments of their time on the dance floor. Ras had such a sexy way of moving his body.

He was swept into the music and the mood, and brought her right along with him. Slim hips that easily swiveled and his strong posture gave his dance moves such a confident air. He was all man without wearing his masculinity in a controlling way. Ras's power was absolute but quiet. It didn't need to shout.

He was as luminous as the moon itself and seemed pleased with this paradise of a yacht he'd chartered. His hair blew in the night, his eyes sparkled and his fine cheek and jaw bones deflected light and shadow. Clearly he'd been upset about something earlier. He'd glossed over it, saying something about a business problem. He was incomprehensible indeed, as she still didn't know what his daily life was like. And probably never would. It really wasn't important, though. She'd found herself on this unexpected journey, but he'd been very clear that he was only in the US for a couple of weeks and had many things to attend to at his unspecified home in Asia.

"Perhaps you'd like to tour the rest of the ship tomorrow?" the captain asked.

"Yes, that's a good idea," Ras agreed.

Back inside the massive master suite, Gracie's attention turned to the bed. The gigantic bed with pillows propped up against a quilted headboard, the piece arranged to look straight forward through the glass panels. There were curtains operated by a remote control to give that particular section of the room even greater privacy and climate control. A bed on the balcony. A bed in the suite. A hot enigma of a man. Gracie's pulse sped up at the thoughts she was having. About how maybe her vow to never be with a man again was too harsh. Maybe there was a man out there for her. Not Ras, but perhaps someone else? Somehow, being with him gave her twinges of loneliness. It reminded her that she had no one to count on. Everyone had abandoned her. Her parents, who came and went without warning. Davis, who wasn't going to make a lifetime commitment to someone he felt so superior to. And then even the product of their union had left her alone, in the most tragic way. Why wasn't she entitled to someone she could trust?

She reminded herself not to let her pleasant exterior fade. Ras was being so generous, the least she could do was be good company. Their midnight snack and warm chamomile tea in heavy stone mugs was a comfort. When they were finished and the wee hours of the night were approaching, Ras rang for David to take

Gracie to her stateroom one deck below, where the guest cabins were.

"Good night, then," she said, with a bit of sadness at being separated from him.

"I had one of the most marvelous days of my life."

She gulped. She could say the same, but the fact that he articulated it shot into her heart like a moonbeam.

"Thank you for this opportunity. I look forward to showing you Savannah tomorrow," she replied.

"Yes."

The finest stateroom on the lower deck had been prepared for her. It was as extravagant as the master suite although, obviously, nowhere near its size. A private balcony, a sitting area, two televisions, a bathroom stocked with amenities. After washing up, she crawled into the comfortable bed. She decided to text Jen and let her know that she was on a yacht named *Destiny* embarking from Miami. Just so that someone in the world would know where she was.

Jen wrote back.

What's his name?

Gracie laughed out loud.

I told you. No attachments.

We'll see.

Jen added an emoji of a face with hearts for eyes, which made Grace giggle again.

Surveying the room from the perspective of the sumptuous bed, she planned to slowly make a mental memory of all of the carefully chosen details of the decor. Instead, she fell asleep replaying the image of dancing with Ras, the way he never once took his eyes off her.

She slept long and soundly. When she woke up, she stepped out on the balcony to see that they had traveled during the early hours and were ported in Savannah, Georgia. She showered and readied herself for the day. A knock on her door was the polite Neo, there to tell her she was expected up in Ras's suite for breakfast.

"This is certainly charming," Ras noted as he and Gracie strolled through Forsyth Park.

"It's one of Savannah's most well-known landmarks."

They approached the central fountain with its tall and wide spray. It was no wonder there were a lot of people taking photos to remember it by. Ras bristled at the number of people and took Gracie's elbow to steer her away, taking notice of her always smooth skin. They could do without a photo or a selfie. Ras was certain he'd remember everything about this trip for the rest of his life. "Tell me about these trees."

"They're oak, dripping with Spanish moss. Savannah is famous for them. They like parks here. There are twenty-two city squares."

"Can we see them all?" Ras was feeling lighthearted this morning. Yesterday's unpleasant news about his fiancée's exploits reminded him that he had so much to attend to when he returned home, including, apparently, helping his future wife to become a proper monarch.

He so appreciated that, unexpectedly, he was accompanied by such a charming companion. Last night after Gracie went to her cabin, he had spent some time in his absurdly large master suite alone idly thinking about her. She had such joie de vivre in her, and it was something he'd been missing in his life for so long now, he'd almost forgotten it existed. He'd never been so drawn to a woman. She absolutely intoxicated him.

As to visiting the city parks, Gracie said, "We have a tee time not long after lunch so we'll choose our sights wisely and see some of them, how about that?"

"Deal."

Last night, Gracie had told Captain Ernesto that their next port out of Miami would be Savannah. So this morning at breakfast, after Ras had expressed an interest in golfing, she'd checked online to find the best course in town and he'd booked it for them. When they were ready to leave, he'd smiled at the look on her face when the captain and crew operated the controls to open the storage compartment on the yacht that housed a Porsche 911 silver sports car. "Are you kidding me!" she'd exclaimed incredulously, in a way that made him laugh. "There's a car too?"

"Ah, the travel professional hasn't seen every level of luxury yet?" he'd teased.

"I have to confess I haven't."

"We'll see what we can do about that," he'd replied in a raspy, sexy voice that he'd never heard coming out of his mouth. How could he help but flirt with her? She was irresistible.

"Savannah has the largest National Historic District in the United States," Gracie said as they continued their walking tour, the car parked in a garage at the moment.

She directed them to a couple of those city squares. They sat down on a bench. The dripping Spanish moss provided not only shade but a sort of hush. He stretched one of his arms across the top of the bench. He sensed her shoulders along his biceps and hand. A battle erupted within him. He wanted to lay that hand on her to bring them closer on the bench. He knew that he shouldn't, yet her body made a shift closer toward him. He sensed it was involuntary and not something she had planned. But she moved her back against his side and, when she did, rockets shot through every blood vessel in his body. Confusing him. If she continued behavior like that, he wasn't sure how long he'd be able to hold out before returning it.

"This is all you promised it would be," he declared a bit later as he scanned the golf course from the elevation of the clubhouse. The whole of the historic downtown was visible from the expansive view. And the course itself, by a world-famous designer, was endless yards of expertly maintained grass and foliage, with canals, ponds and a central lake, pristine in the afternoon sunshine.

"Founded in 1930, it's always been considered one of the best courses in America."

While Ras requested they walk from hole to hole, Gracie had booked a premier package and they were assigned a caddy who followed them in a cart holding the clubs they'd rented. The fresh air and grass reminded him of the palace grounds, of blissful years running around with Lucky on those manicured lawns, his mother giving him license to play and get dirty.

"Do you golf much?" he asked.

"Not until recently. I took lessons because I figured it was something future clients might be interested in."

He so admired that despite the rough times she'd endured, she was moving forward with her life. Chasing her dream. What a unique woman she was. "You?"

"Oh, yes, lessons as a child. My mother liked a lot of sports. Said it was good for the brains as well as the brawn." She chuckled at the cute expression. "In fact, some of my favorite memories are of golfing with her. Just the two of us. Sometimes we'd only take two clubs and just whack the ball toward each other like it had become a game of ice hockey. Just to be silly and to laugh. My mother was good at laughing."

He went silent for a moment as his words pulled his gravity downward. If only he could look forward to a future as happy as his past had been. He knew that wasn't likely, that he and Vajhana might ultimately be able to find a working alliance, save for marriage vows, but they'd never have the sheer family joy that filled the palace when Queen Sirind ran barefoot through the halls.

The caddy presented them with tall plastic glasses. Inside was sweet and icy tea, most welcome after they'd traversed the green. He watched Gracie sip, feeling more connected to her than he had to anyone in his life. She got him thinking about every subject under the sun. Somehow, in the middle of the golf course, he was having memories that hadn't occurred to him in years. She was a splash of color bursting into his black-and-white heart. They stood close as they drank, appreciating their surroundings. Pulled by a supernatural force, he bent his face closer to her, just as he had on the park bench when she'd inched her body just a perceptible bit toward his. Her full lips glistened from the sweet drink. He wanted to taste those lips. Maybe just once. Or maybe until eternity. Then he leaned in a little farther still, until their mouths were only inches away from each other. He could all but feel her breath.

He startled himself, came to his senses and backed off.

Did he notice a little sign of disappointment on her pretty face?

CHAPTER SIX

HAD RAS BEEN about to *kiss* her? Gracie couldn't stop replaying the moment on the ninth hole when they'd stopped for a glass of iced tea. As they stood together and surveyed the golf course, it seemed like he had been moving toward her. If she was being honest, she'd have to admit to herself that she absolutely, desperately, emphatically wanted him to kiss her. Even though she knew it wouldn't have meant anything other than succumbing to a momentary urge.

Just as when they'd sat on that bench and he seemed to be putting his arm around her. Her body, without being asked to, had brought itself closer against his, all of her molecules questioning *what-if*? It was all just dalliance, but she couldn't stop herself. Obviously, she and Ras could never be together. He deserved a real, live, enduring love, and that was something she could never give him. Her scars would never heal. She still didn't have a picture of his life, but when he spoke of his mother she could tell that only someone capable of great love could be capable of the great hurt he'd suffered by her loss.

After they'd finished the eighteenth hole, they returned to the pro shop to check the clubs back in and settle the account. Gracie idled around in the shop, browsing the sunglasses and hats. Along one wall of the shop were shelves with a nice selection of international newspapers and magaz—

What? She couldn't believe her eyes. They must have been deceiving her. She glanced back to Ras who she could see in profile as he spoke with the club manager. And then her eyes shot back to the publications. To Ras, then to the third shelf of the display. To Ras, then to the magazine called *World's Young Royals*. To Ras, then to the photo that took up half of the cover, a man in full royal regalia identified as His Royal Highness Crown Prince Rasmayada of Ko Pha Lano. The second half of the cover showed a photo of a woman with long dark hair in a revealing designer dress that left nothing to the imagination. She drank from an open bottle of champagne in one hand and her other arm was thrown around a blond-haired man who had a royal sash over his jacket, named as a British earl, Lord Cyril. The caption read: Prince Ras and Princess Vajhana: On or Off?

Gracie couldn't make sense of the information overload. She'd known he was a person of notoriety, he'd all but told her so. But a royal? After he settled up at the counter, he found her and froze in front of the magazine cover as well. She could hear him swallow before he whispered, "Let's get out of here."

The valet had brought the Porsche to the exit, so they quickly got in. Ras pulled out onto the gravel road as they headed back to the main street. Gracie was seeing stars; she simply couldn't bring her thoughts together. "You're a prince?"

"Yes."

"A prince. Like with a crown and a throne?"

He smiled. "Theoretically, that won't be until my father dies and I become king, but yes."

"A prince of an island in the Gulf of Thailand who boarded a public cruise in New York?"

"I wanted to travel without being noticed. As you can see from the magazine cover, and you'll find on numerous websites, people's fascination with royalty can be oppressive."

"So, when you spoke before of your family business…"

"Yes, I meant that my father is sort of the CEO and I'm next in command."

"And about that *merger* you got some bad news about?"

"Yes, well, as you saw on the magazine cover, I'm to be married."

As they traveled back to the harbor, among her many emotions was hurt that he hadn't told her who he was sooner. And especially about the woman he was to *merge* with. Not that it should be any concern of hers. Except, somehow it was. She'd pressed her body into his, he'd almost kissed her, or so she'd sensed. And everything that had come before. The smiles that told her he'd been pleased when they kept running into each other on the cruise, the sharing of chocolates, the dancing that was unmistakably sensual.

He'd mentioned being recognizable and was always looking around as if he suspected he was being followed. She supposed he didn't want to be photographed alone in the US if he was engaged to be *merged*. Although from the looks of the princess, she didn't seem to share the same worry. Still, it all stung. That he didn't trust her enough to tell her who he really was, didn't think she was worthy of the information. It made perfect sense from his point of view. Irrationally, it hit her like a rejection.

"As you could see from the cover photos, my arranged marriage to be is a bit of a sham."

"Arranged marriage, crowns, do you have a scepter, too?" She sounded a bit snitty so restrained herself. There was no logical reason to take offense. She hadn't told him everything about herself, either. "How do you feel about a wife being chosen for you?"

"I have an obligation to my people and she to hers. Our marriage will be part of our jobs and never anything more."

There was something wistful in the words he said, singed around the edges with sadness. Maybe even longing. Something she well understood. For all her proclamations about a life untethered, she knew that was going to be a lonesome path. Especially since she still longed for something that was taken from her forever. Her palm went to her belly.

"The business *merger* you talked about."

"Yes, a collaborative effort of both of our fathers to a large agenda of bringing manufacturing to the islands."

"Whereas you think developing eco-friendly tourism is a better idea."

"Yes. Marine conservation, for starters."

"There's a big interest in voluntourism."

"I know. I have to convince my father not to go forward with their plans."

"What does your fiancée think?"

"What did it look like on the magazine cover? She has no interest. But she's going to at least need to keep her unprincess-like behavior out of the media or we'll both end up humiliated. Our engagement was only announced to the press months ago."

"I don't know anything about your royal rules but, of course, you don't want photos like that one splashed across the news." Ras shook his head in distress, like he was at a loss. So was she, for a different reason. Somehow, learning he was a renowned captain of industry or some other reason for his fame would be far easier to fathom than him being a prince. But, okay, she was on a voyage with His Royal Highness. This was a once-in-a lifetime experience in so many ways.

"I'm so sorry. I was just trying to have a little getaway on my own before I got married, as my mother wanted me to. I've been trying to keep all of this under wraps. At first I thought my father was having me followed to either force me home or track my every move. But by this point, I doubt that. Then there's the possibility of being recognized by the general public who'd love to snap a compromising shot and sell it to the press. On top of that are the ruthless bona fide paparazzi relentlessly trying to get any juice they can. The photo of me on that magazine cover is one of my official portraits, but Vajhana on the lap of an earl is a fresh catch."

They parked the car at the harbor. When they reached the yacht, Ras handed the fob to Neo who would return the car to the boat. Gracie felt like she was being pulled with the tide, from the golf shop to the car to the harbor and now onto the yacht.

"Did you have a good day of sightseeing?" Captain Ernesto asked as he welcomed them back onto the ship.

"Fine," Ras said brusquely.

"Do you still desire dinner onboard?"

"Yes." They'd talked about it earlier because Gracie thought it would be nice if they took a night sail to look at Hilton Head and Myrtle Beach islands. And they'd decided to make it a dinner cruise. In the morning they'd head northward to their next destination.

"Shall I have two masseuses come aboard in an hour for massages in the spa?"

"Yes."

"May I show you the activities deck where the spa is located? Since you arrived late last night, you didn't have a chance to see it."

"Fine." She knew Ras well enough by now to perceive from his tight voice and straightened eyebrows that he was still rattled about the magazine cover. A massage should help. Although she could hardly blame him for being upset. It was sad that the only way he could find some peace and reconciliation about marrying a woman he didn't love was to steal away on a secret trip away from her.

As Captain Ernesto led them to the activities deck, Gracie continued to be impressed by the details of the yacht. It was, indeed, meant for royalty. "The cinema," the captain said as he ushered them into a theater. Gracie quickly counted twelve plush red-velvet-covered reclining chairs. Between each was a small wood table for refreshments. Behind those recliners were a couple of rows of traditional movie theater seats, which Gracie figured came into use if there were additional guests. A glass snack bar lined one of the walls. It held a popcorn machine and a soda dispenser, and underneath the glass were shelves full of popular movie theater candy. The screen itself was theater-size, framed by a red velvet curtain that matched the chairs.

There was a fitness studio, a clean room with exercise equipment positioned to face seaward and several screens directed at different angles for video entertainment while working out. Weights, yoga mats and Pilates apparatus were at the ready. "When you'd like to participate in water sports, I'll be delighted to show you our equipment."

"Thank you."

Next, he showed them a party room, a large space with a hardwood dance floor and cocktail tables set up along the windows. Gracie could imagine whoever was chartering the boat hosting events onboard. The captain opened a pair of wooden double doors. "And here is our chapel." A white room, with wallpaper that depicted delicate cherry blossoms, held six white upholstered pews. Two simple chandeliers gave the room a special feel without being over the top. The floors were lushly carpeted, and at the front of the room stood a white pulpit. Behind it were windows to provide beautiful views.

Ras took a deep inhale. Gracie imagined he was considering his own upcoming nuptials. She was sure his royal wedding would be a massive affair with hundreds or maybe even thousands in attendance. What a unique agony was his fate. She wondered, for only a quick minute, what it would be like to be his bride. This man who made her feel so good about herself. A man she could talk and listen to for hours on end. With whom she could share everything she felt, without fear of uninterest and belittlement. Not to mention after the brushes of physical contact they'd had, she imagined what his big hands would feel like on her, how his full lips would be pressed against hers.

She forced all of those thoughts away with what felt like a literal push. She could have just as easily ended up standing at the altar with Davis. After being so ignored and irrelevant to her parents, she'd been desperate for Davis's attention. In the beginning, she would have married him in a minute. He'd looked like stability, someone with whom to build a life, to raise a family. She'd been such a poor judge of character, so hungry for care that it took her a while to notice that he didn't regard her well. How he'd talked down to her, always reminding her of her miserable childhood, telling her she was fortunate he took pity on her. Until he didn't even do that and, after receiving the news of what would be their next step, he'd walked out on her. Thank heavens she never got as far as wearing his ring.

Ras turned his back and headed out of the chapel. That wouldn't be a part of the ship either one of them would need to return to. "We'll see the rest another time, Ernesto. Kindly take us to the spa."

The spa was as carefully designed as the rest of the yacht. Done in a tropical motif, both tall and low-lying green plants were everywhere, creating a dense lushness. A waterfall feature provided nature's music, not a gush, just a gentle rain of drops that instantly lowered his blood pressure whether he'd willed it to or not. Within that space, Gracie looked so pretty, like a mythical creature in her natural habitat. It had annoyed him that on seeing the chapel, his mind had immediately gone to Vajhana and the disappointment that he'd probably be dealt over and over again in his coming life with her. The kind of love his parents had was not to be his. Making the chapel feel like a charade with its promise of true marriage. But somehow when his thoughts returned to Gracie, it was as if a ray of light penetrated through the dark, filling him with hope.

Her radiance was becoming a safe aura for

him to bask in. She'd been open with him, prompting him to want to give her that kind of candor in return. Yet what had he chosen in return? Deception and secrecy. He should have told her who he was sooner, should have gauged that she'd hold his confidence. For her to find out by accident was insulting. He wished he hadn't let it play out that way. Although her finally knowing was like a long sigh of relief. He took her hand, whether he should have or not, to walk around the spa and see its unique features. Resting areas featured furniture in a leafy print fabric. He commented, "It definitely feels like stepping into a different world." In more ways than one.

They turned to an inner alcove. "I like how they made the salon chairs that would be used for hair styling or facial treatments look integrated, like you'd find them in nature." The tools and products were probably behind the closed wood cabinets.

Beyond a wall of bamboo were two massage tables, surrounded by flowering plants emitting their sweet fragrance. A disturbing thought crashed through what would otherwise be a blissful tableau. Were he and Gracie about to get side-by-side massages on those tables? Massages. Where people were generally naked.

Captain Ernesto asked, "Are you ready for Ovia and Coro to begin?"

Now or never, Ras thought with a smile to himself. "Certainly."

"While they set up, if you'd like to use the changing rooms—" he gestured to a wooden door "—you'll find robes and slippers as well as showers and towels. After the massages, I highly recommend the rain forest shower with its ten water jets, built for two."

Ras's gut, or maybe it was lower, twitched at the idea of sharing a shower for two with Gracie. She lowered her eyes as well, obviously uncomfortable at the suggestion. First the park bench, then the almost-kiss at the golf course? What was he thinking? Although, he considered, as a wicked thrill washed through him, why not? The *why not* was that it wouldn't be fair to Gracie. Perhaps it was part of his journey, of this whole escape, to fully fathom and accept what he and Vajhana were, and weren't, going to have. To find his place in it. Maybe, but not with Gracie. They'd already reached such a forbidden closeness that he knew it was going to be wrenching to say goodbye when this was all over. It would be a terrible mistake to make that any worse for both of them.

There was no scenario that could keep them

together. Even if he wasn't engaged and she wasn't closed off to a romantic relationship, he was no different from that snob Davis who thought Gracie was too far beneath him. Ras's mother was a commoner, but from a wealthy and thoroughbred family. Crown Prince Ras had to marry for his country; he couldn't just marry *anyone*. That was a fight he would never win.

He and Gracie entered the spa's dressing areas, and he was glad to see there were *his* and *her* sections with the aforementioned grand shower between them. He took off his clothes, imagining Gracie doing the same on the other side. Was she in front of the mirror at the vanity table, as conscious of her nakedness as he was his? The erection that reflected back at him was powerful. Not needing the validation his title bestowed on him. A man and a woman, stripped to their essence. What soul-searching might they share and wounds might they salve if they allowed themselves to? He'd never know.

"Ready?" she called across the shower. They met in the middle, both in thick, white terry-cloth robes.

The masseuses were waiting for them in the massage area, two uniformed women with their hair pulled tightly back. "If you'd like to lie down on the tables, madam and sir," one said with a gesture. They both assisted Ras and Gracie onto the tables, shrouding them with sheets as they took their robes off, affording much modesty. Although as he fit his face into the headrest he was keenly aware of Gracie beside him.

"This feels amazing," he heard Gracie coo as her treatment commenced. Her voice coated him in equal measure to the scented massage oil being applied to his shoulders. You *feel amazing*, was what he wanted to say in return but, of course, didn't. As the massage went on, he was washed over and over again with Gracie's declarations of pleasure. His only regret was that he wasn't eliciting them from her himself.

After an expert combination of Eastern and Western bodywork techniques, the masseuse helped him back into his robe. It took all of his concentration not to turn to watch Gracie doing the same.

They moved to a terrace to relax in reclining chairs. She eased into one and pushed it all the way back until it was in a V shape. "I love these zero gravity chairs. They take all the pressure off your back."

"Yes, we have some on various balconies at the palace." He sat down and pushed the seat back to its full recline.

She giggled. "That probably feels very natural coming out of your mouth. But you can imagine how unusual that sounds to me." She used an exaggerated fancy voice, "Oh, yes, I held a charity ball at the palace last night."

"Is that how I sound?" he teased.

"No, but you get my point."

"Indeed," he laughed.

"There you go again. No one says *indeed* in real life."

"You better watch yourself, smart mouth." Indeed, *indeed*, did she have a smart mouth. Not to mention sexy, the way her two lips parted slightly in repose. He'd come so close to kissing said smart mouth before and was ready to pounce upon her zero-gravity chair right now. Of course, those were only fleeting thoughts he would never act upon. But Gracie's uninhibited way about her made him want to act the same. "Once again, I'm sorry I withheld my identity from you. Every time we ran into each other on the cruise I assumed it was the last, and then it just snowballed."

"I guess there's nothing we can do about that

now, Your Royal Highness." Her good humor was appreciated.

Once they returned to the dressing area, the rain forest shower for two still stood tauntingly at the ready. He summoned his self-control as the dilemma had an obvious solution. He couldn't be expected to get into that shower with her and not sponge her shapely body, an activity that he thought might take him hours. A force had genuinely begun inside him as he found more thoughts than not had become about her. But he wouldn't treat her as she had become unfortunately used to, cast aside when no longer needed. He had to keep things to the acquaintanceship they'd settled on, a friendly tourist and tour guide who happened to open up their souls to each other, a rare occurrence in the world.

"Please, you take this rain forest shower and observe all of its features. I can tell you, extravagant personal care facilities like this are definitely something the high-end traveler wants."

"What will *you* do?"

"There are other showers in the men's changing room. I'll meet you back in the relaxation area. Take your time and enjoy yourself." Two things he'd like to be doing. With her.

He proceeded to shower and dress. When she

exited the changing room door to reunite with him, she was a vision. Her wet hair was tousled and her skin positively glowed, as if it had been kissed by the sun. "How was the shower?"

"Exquisite. You absolutely have to try it while we're aboard."

He was unable to shut down ideas of making it an activity for two. "I'll take it on your recommendation."

She poured them two glasses of the coconut water that had been provided and he grabbed a bowl with dried fruits and nuts. They sat down in front of the waterfall on another one of those sofas that were large enough to be beds, probably seated more intimately than they should have been, yet they were there before he'd had a chance to decide against it.

"This is really divine, Ras." He swallowed. Looking into those light brown eyes, he fell into a trance. He was quite sure he could stare at her for an indefinite period of time. Maybe forever. "Can I have some of those snacks?"

He picked the plumpest almond out of the bowl. Pinching it between two fingers, he used it to slowly outline her lips, which parted in acceptance of the sensation. After he made a circle all the way around her mouth he placed his fingers ever so slightly against her lips and watched her tongue dart to grab the nut. A slight smile moved across her face as she chewed. "That tasted especially good."

"Do you want another?" a voice so low it was almost a roar came out of him.

"Yes, please."

This time he selected a Brazil nut, smooth on its surface. It's bigger size glided along the fullness of her lips. She bit it in two as he fed it to her, his body vibrating as if it were a guitar with strings that had been plucked. "More?"

"Delicious." He directly fed a couple of dried cranberries onto her tongue.

And then rational thought couldn't hold him back any longer and he leaned over to replace his lips for the snacks. Her mouth was plush and tender. The tip of his tongue explored in the same circle the nuts had before. Then the fullness of his lips pressed into hers. Those guitar strings thrummed inside him. Which urged him forward to seal their mouths together as the kisses became longer. Their lips opened and her sweet taste was as divine as he'd envisioned it would be. He brought a hand up to caress her cheek, coaxing her even closer to him. He dotted her entire face with kisses, his lips hardly knowing where to go first.

His mouth found the furrow of her neck, pro-

voking a tiny moan from her. Tracing down to
the hollow of her throat, he breathed into the
smell of her skin. Back up to her mouth, which
he had to take again and again, starving for
more and more still. His fingers laced through
the velvet strands that were her hair.

"Gracie," he murmured softly but, really, it
was a flag speared into the dirt. A claim. A
home.

That was probably a mistake, Gracie thought in
her cabin as she dressed for dinner. Succumbing to Ras's considerable appeal and feeling
bonded to him after all they'd shared over the
last couple of days, she had no strength to deny
the kisses that he'd instigated, yet both wanted.
Genuine, robust and urgent. His kisses came
from the heavens, they belonged to the universe, pure demonstrations of human emotion
that could not be bound by logic. They were so
monumental, they had to be honored. She felt
them down into her core, like no kisses she had
ever received or given before, and the fact was
she wanted more.

"You look stunning," he said as she came
up the last stairs leading from her cabin to his.
While she didn't have a lot of clothes with her,
originally thinking she was only on a cruise

for a few nights from New York to Miami and back, she was glad she hadn't yet worn the dress she had on now. It was black with a halter tie at the neck, the front plunging low. It was long, past her ankles, and fit slimly all the way down. She thought of it as her glamour dress, and she felt sexy in it. A long gold chain and a pair of hoop earrings added to the look that she finished with black platform sandals and a shimmery gold wrap in case it got cold in the night air.

"May I serve you a first course?" David appeared wielding a tray. A formal table had been set for them with a fine brocade tablecloth and napkins in cobalt blue. Polished silverware was arranged for several courses. A bottle of champagne chilled in a metal ice bucket on a stand. An arrangement of purple and blue flowers made for a vivid centerpiece.

"Shall we?" Ras gestured to Gracie, and they approached the table. He pulled out a chair for her, and she sat as he pushed it in. He then took the chair opposite. They were extraordinarily comfortable for dining chairs with cushioned armrests. Gracie took note of how painstakingly they must have been chosen.

David moved in to lift the champagne out of the bucket and wait for Ras's nod of approval at the label. He popped the cork with the most minimal sound, the measure of an experienced server. Pouring the bubbly into two flutes, he immediately retreated from the table to allow the two of them a private toast.

"To adventure."

"Adventure." They clinked their crystal and sipped.

Once they'd had a few minutes, David returned with two plates. "Heirloom tomatoes from the farmers' market in Savannah." Gracie liked the detail of the specific place where the tomatoes were purchased. While she and Ras were sightseeing and golfing, the crew was attending to their voyage, including buying things like tomatoes and fresh flowers.

The artfully arranged plate contained yellow, orange and brown-hued tomatoes. "The drizzle of balsamic reduction really brings out their sweetness," Ras commented.

They chatted a bit about the agriculture on Ko Pha Lano. "Have you heard about the mineral accretion technologies?" she asked. "There are coral reef restoration programs that use low-voltage electrical currents to aid the health and growth of coral reefs and other marine life."

"Yes. Other islands in the gulf are doing that. And we need more farming. The massive amount of importation we do for food and other goods drives prices up, contributing to the stagnant economy."

"Hence the manufacturing industries the two kings want to bring in as a solution."

"Honestly, I don't think my father truly understands how the island never fully recovered from my mother's death."

"How so?" she asked as she speared her fork into a tomato.

"The mood, the disposition of the entire nation. Which is now transferring down to the children of the subjects who were of my mother's era."

"She sounds like both an accomplished queen and an amazing mother."

A smile broke on one side of his mouth. Yet there was a glint of sorrow in his eyes. "She was. Her monthly addresses from the palace balcony drew thousands."

David replaced their appetizer plates with the main course. "Grilled crab legs, corn *elote* with chili, lime and cotija cheese. And sauteed fresh spinach."

"Thank you." Ras nodded and dismissed him.

"What did she talk to your people about?"

"That was what was so wonderful. She spoke about both civic and ordinary things. A success

I might have had at school. A challenge to one of our districts, such as roadwork that was creating a traffic problem. A benefit concert she was organizing. She had such innate humanity. I think it was because she was a commoner. She understood the lives of people outside the palace."

"You said that's why she wanted you to take this trip."

"Yes, and she set aside a fund for me to do so, that I shouldn't spend the nation's money on my own pursuits."

"She was thoughtful."

"Yes, and my father's approach to ruling is nothing like hers. He dutifully keeps the needs of his subjects foremost in his mind, but he's icy and distant. Especially after my mother died. He hardened."

"What a terrible tragedy you both endured."

"As have you, from what you told me. Parents who basically abandoned you, and a fool of a man who didn't treat you as the precious jewel you are."

Gracie all but swooned. Those words were like balms to parched skin. Ras had a way of making her feel so valued. Fate had dealt her a cruel irony in meeting a man like him, a man she couldn't have.

"I haven't yet told you about my loss far greater than that."

He tilted his head, intrigued. "Go on."

There was no reason not to confide in him. "I became pregnant with Davis's child." Her hand reflexively went to her belly, as it had thousands of times before. "He told me I wasn't the kind of woman he and his family would want to continue the family name. That the best thing would be for me to get rid of it."

"*Get rid of it?* What does that even mean?"

"I suppose that I should either have an abortion or that I should give the baby up for adoption so there would be no connection to his or her true parentage."

Ras gritted his teeth. "What a disgusting human."

"I didn't want to do either of those. When that became obvious, Davis left and told me never to get in touch with him ever again. And that if I ever told the child who his or her father was, he'd crush me under his heel. Those were his exact words."

Ras reached across the table to cover her hand with his, so big and strong. He caressed her with the pad of his thumb, back and forth in a tender and soothing motion. "I can't even imagine the abandonment you must have felt."

"That wasn't all of it."

"You had to endure more?"

"Weeks after Davis left, I had a miscarriage. That was the pinnacle. There's no loss, no desertion, that could be worse than that."

CHAPTER SEVEN

A WAVE OF sorrow crashed over Ras at Gracie's admission. She was right, there was nothing more tragic than a parent losing their child. Even the child they'd never met, one who was growing inside his or her mother. "Gracie, I'm so sorry."

As they'd finished their entrée, Ras stood up and moved to her side of the table. Her face had taken on a pallor so unlike her usual glow. He was glad that she didn't try to hide it from him.

"Let's walk around the deck," she requested.

They strolled the perimeter. She held his hand, and he had no intention of letting it go unless she wanted him to. It seemed she had more to say to him, and he wanted to give her the opportunity to do so. "You said Davis had already left you when you miscarried. What was his reaction?" he asked gently.

"He didn't know, Ras. It happened a few

weeks after he'd thrown me out of his house in Point Pleasant. After he'd confirmed how small and insignificant I was to him, I got the bus station job in Newark. He never found out I lost the child he wanted me to *get rid of.* It ended up as what he wanted, not having a child with me, but he never found out why."

"Why didn't you tell him?"

"What difference did it make? I couldn't stay with him after all of that."

Ras shook his head in disbelief. "You're surely better off without him."

"I am."

"And you didn't tell your parents, either?"

"No. I couldn't have even if I wanted to."

"Why not?"

"I had no idea where they were. I still don't."

Her words caused another stab to Ras's heart. He squeezed her hand as they stopped along the portside railing, with very few lights illuminating the area. They peered out at the ocean in its darkness. The sound of the water crashed like a symphony.

"Gracie, you've been through so much. How are you so resilient?"

"I don't know that I am. If I've learned anything, it's that I can only count on myself. That I'll never fall in love with anyone ever again.

I'll never rely on someone else." Something about that tugged at Ras. In the strangest way, he wanted her to rely on him. He knew he'd never betray her. He could give her the solid ground that she deserved to stand on. To walk through life never trusting anyone was a horrible fate. It was one he faced, too. His matrimony to Vajhana was not to be built on trust or honor. It was concocted for purpose.

"What happened after you moved to Newark?"

"I got a tiny apartment. After work and on the weekends, I started taking classes in the travel sector. And slowly but consistently, I learned and formulated my outline for the rest of my life." Her certainty about an existence without love tapped against Ras's chest. Because he'd decided on the same thing. He'd marry the princess, he'd produce an heir, he'd serve his people. Yet in the process he would become like his father, not the joyous mother who had exuberance for life and living. There was no point in lamenting; that was the path in front of him. Just as Gracie had decided on hers.

She turned her head to make eye contact with him. Her hair whipped around her face in a wild storm. Her lips were ripe and plump. He swooped down and brought his hands underneath her hair, to the back of her neck. And then all of a sudden his lips pressed into hers and he was kissing her again. "Gracie, Gracie. You make me wish for things that are impossible."

When she lifted her arms up and around his shoulders, yearning coursed through him. His hands slid down her sides and to her waist, where he pulled her tightly against him, wanting to shore up any gaps between their two bodies. With her back against the ship's railing, he moved into her, a crush of their bodies with every kiss, using the groove he created with her in the Cuban nightclub of Miami. But now they provided the melody themselves in a dance only for them. And the ocean. And the moonlight. And the heavens.

His lips brushed against one cheek and then the other, her skin like milled talcum. She made many utterances of pleasure that were like kisses to him. His hands slid from her waist, along her hips. Blood rushed to his center as he pressed into her, stiffening him to steel. Tomorrow no longer mattered. Of course, he could have no future with this enchanting and emotional woman. Both had decisions they'd made and both had barriers. Although, if she was willing, they could have this moment, easily the most exciting of his life.

Suddenly, he was picking her up and into his arms, carrying her along the deck, the smashing sound of each wave urging him on. The wind billowed his white shirt into a sail as her warm lips furrowed into his neck. With a kick, he opened the aft entrance to his suite. Striding across the room to his opulent master bed, he whispered to her, "Can we be together tonight? I want you so much."

"I do, too, Ras," came the answer he needed to hear.

He looked at her lying curved in the center of his bed, a magnificent sight. "The only thing that could look better than you do right now would be if you were naked."

Although the panes of glass surrounding his suite were completely privacy darkened and no one could see in, he grabbed the remote control to shut the curtains that surrounded the room, making their lair all the more only theirs, even hiding from the Atlantic. When he assured himself that operation was complete, he retrieved the condoms he'd wistfully noticed in the toiletry basket beside the sink. Then when he turned his attention back to Gracie, his breath caught in surprise. She'd done exactly what he'd stated as his wish. Her clothes were in a pile on the floor. She'd quickly removed them and lay there naked with a sly smile, one arm propping her up, her head leaning back a bit, all of it forming the most seductive S-shape ever in the world. His eyes glazed.

"Is this what you had in mind?" she purred.

"Oh, yes, I was right. This is even better than that sexy black dress you had on."

He snaked onto the bed to join her. One hand slid ever so slowly across her hair, down her face along her jawline, into the crook of her throat. With no reason to stop there, his thumb traced her shoulder along her arm down to her fingertips, which led him across her hips and to her thigh. He felt behind her knee and then down the rest of her leg to her foot. Every part of the exploration was magnificent, if one-sided as he made a mental note to remember the other side of her body next time his hands made their travels. And there would be many next times; in fact he couldn't keep his touch off her skin. His hand cupped her breast, so pliant and creamy that his second hand had to have the other one. He held them, reveling at their perfect fit in his palms. Until the tips of his fingers became itchy to caress and pull on her nipples, making them hard with just a few satisfying strokes. As he did, her head fell back and a slow, delicious moan vibrated from her throat.

His mouth found hers and their tongues wrote more music together, one he knew he'd replay in his memories for the rest of his life. He couldn't get enough of this woman. She was in his blood. In every inhale and every exhale. He'd never imagined the affinity he felt with her, the tie. And to bring that joining to the physical as they did now, in perfect sync, was a gift from the hereafter.

His hands explored every vertebra of her spine. Hers searched to untuck his shirt from his pants, sliding her hands underneath to make contact. The hairs on each inch of his body stood on end at her electrifying touch, skin to skin. She unbuttoned his shirt, slowly, tantalizingly, to place her palms flat against his chest. Next, her hands roamed over him, learning him. Any way she touched him was ecstasy. He wanted to give himself to her completely. He gasped when she reached into his pants and wrapped her delicate fingers around his hardness. Quickly unzipping his fly he worked his pants down, all the while her supple hand swelling him more than he'd ever thought possible, coursing him with not want but need.

Finally naked as she was, their arms and legs tangled into one creature, desperately taking and giving with their hands and mouths until no part of either was neglected.

When he couldn't take it any longer, he rolled her onto her back, sheathed the condom onto himself and got on top of her. His knees urged hers open as he angled himself to enter her. Only one inch at first as he wanted to read her body and her face. Her smile encouraged him and he slipped farther into her.

"That feels so good, Ras." When he entered her all the way, she cried out in arousal as he centered himself and fastened to her. Despite her sounds of pleasure, she couldn't possibly know the rhapsody and rapture she was causing his body and soul.

They rocked, at first gently and then not so gently. Slow and deliberate, and alternately fast and frenzied. They rode each other like the high tides of the ocean surrounding them, the ebb and flow, over and over and over again. Until it crested them over and they crashed, grasping each other like life preservers.

The next morning, Gracie took Ras to the breakfast restaurant that she'd selected for them in the Charleston City Market. Within the two-hundred-year-old brick buildings, over three hundred shops and restaurants attracted visitors from all over the world. She'd read about this particular restaurant and had decided that would be their first stop of the day. Captain Ernesto had known that he was to set off from Savannah early in the morning for their brief stop at the historic city of Charleston in nearby South Carolina.

She'd spoken to Captain Ernesto last night. Before dinner. Before heirloom tomato salads. Before she'd told Ras her most painful truth. Before the walk on the moonlit deck. And before they'd retired to private quarters to discuss things further. Er, that was to say communicated in a non-verbal way. One that had left her feeling boneless and dazed this morning. Even as they strolled arm in arm through the colorful streets of Charleston.

"Good morning. Breakfast for two?" the hostess asked as they came into the cheery restaurant.

Gracie responded, "Yes, and if you have a table by the window, that would be great."

"Follow me." She sat them at a lovely table in its own little alcove that overlooked the comings and goings of the famous old marketplace. "Is this your first visit to Charleston?"

"Yes."

"I'll send your waitress right over," the hostess said with a big-toothed smile, making Gracie glad that she'd chosen this restaurant known for its southern charm. The open room with its white tablecloths and wooden ceiling fans was a lovely destination from where to start the day. And before the waitress could arrive, the hostess returned with a pot of hot coffee that she poured into the red porcelain mugs on the table. She laid down a basket. "These are our mini biscuits. Looks like today we have pimento cheese, blackberry and buttermilk." Ras and Gracie looked at each other with a smile, silently agreeing that hot biscuits served with soft butter was a quite appealing way to start their morning. Of course, their morning had already begun back in his bedroom suite. In fact, appetites had been satiated starting at dawn, but that was a different hunger entirely. Ras winked at her as if he was remembering their earlier activities as well.

When the waitress arrived to greet them, Gracie took charge. "We'll both have shrimp and grits."

"Good choice. Anything else I can get you?"

"Not at the moment, thanks." Once she walked away Gracie said enthusiastically to

Ras, "That's a historic dish down in the Low-country, as they call it."

"You surely do your homework," he said as his mouth caressed the rim of his mug to take a sip. Lucky mug, she thought to herself. She could watch his lips all day long, so full and expressive. Those lips had wanted to know everything about her last night and again this morning. They knew how to coax a reaction out of just about every spot on her body. The crook of her elbow. On a shoulder blade. Her hip bone. Ras was an intense lover, completely focusing on either the giving or receiving he was involved in. It had been a night and morning of lovemaking like she'd never known existed.

Although, she was well aware of what it didn't mean, too. When the food arrived, she took one bite of the juicy seafood forked up with the buttery grains of the grits. And then put her fork down to state plainly, just to get it out of the way. "Ras, I know what happened between us last night and this morning didn't mean anything."

"You're wrong. It meant a lot."

"Thank you. What I'm trying to say is that I understand that we'll say goodbye forever at the end of this trip. You'll tread your path and I'll go mine."

His face turned somber. "Don't ever think that it will have been easy for me."

A corner of her mouth ticked up. "No. We stumbled upon something really special in each other, didn't we? Maybe that's why we can't have it forever. It's like a meteor that shines so bright it has to explode."

"So, we'll have this time together. Let's make the most of it."

"And then it won't be as hard to part as it could be because we'll know that's how it was supposed to end up. We'll be ready for it."

"I have to marry by contract, and you'll never marry at all."

"You see, it's all decided already." Neither of them believed a word they were saying, but it was probably useful to state.

He bent across the table to bring his mouth to hers. His kisses swirled her insides, hypnotizing her, like she could get lost in them and lose all track of time and space. "It's a shame though," he whispered in between, "because I think I might like to kiss you for the rest of my life." They narrowed their eyes at each other, as if someone had issued a dare. Until he broke the eye lock and proclaimed, "Now about these biscuits."

After breakfast, they strolled through the

market, taking special note of the artisans who sat weaving sweetgrass baskets from the local marshland. "It's a tradition of African Americans who live in the Lowcountry and speak the Creole language of Gullah."

"Shall we buy some?"

"As souvenirs?"

Ras realized what he'd just suggested. It wasn't as if he could return to Ko Pha Lano with armfuls of gifts for his father and fiancée. "Let me buy some for you, then."

"No, but thank you. Remember, I'm a nomad now. I have nothing to put in baskets."

"Look," he said, pointing to some very tiny ones. "Surely you'll have a use for a small one like that. You can use it to hold my kisses."

Her lungs swelled at the specialness of that thought. And in sadness because that was all she'd have of him, an empty basket filled with clandestine kisses. "Okay. We'll get one for you, too."

"And why don't we buy some larger ones for the yacht crew."

After the purchases Gracie suggested, "Let's go look at Rainbow Row."

"Wonderful. What's that?"

Once they turned onto the street she intended, Ras had his answer. The Georgian-style houses were painted in pastel colors one after the other. "The most well-known street in Charleston."

"I can see why."

Later, they walked back to the yacht where the basket gifts were appreciated. As they entered Ras's suite, which had been cleaned and the bed made up with fresh linen, Gracie said, "Our next port is Washington, DC."

Ras's brows furrowed. "I shouldn't spend much time in the capital. I've been there too many times for official functions." Was he still concerned that the paparazzi would catch him? Worried that someone would see him on his bachelor freedom quest and post it on a gossip site or in a magazine? She admired that he didn't want to bring any shame to his family. They had a reputation of propriety dating back generations.

"Okay, we'll just go to touristy places, and you can wear your most casual clothes that you bought on *Liberation*."

"Yes… I'm sure that will be…okay."

"We're at sea tomorrow," Gracie reminded Ras even though he hadn't forgotten.

"Yes—" he scratched his chin "—however

will we pass the time?" He winked at her and was gratified by the smile he got in return.

"Well, for this evening, how about we watch a movie?"

After they changed into comfortable clothes, they made their way to the cinema they'd only taken a quick look at. David prepared a popcorn buffet with buttered, cheese and caramel flavors. He also made them mini hotdogs, soft pretzels and put an array of sodas on ice. Ras and Gracie plopped onto the center seats that were the best in the auditorium. "Now, what to watch?"

"Action movie?" Gracie suggested.

"Or comedy?"

"No weepy dramas. I want total escape."

David made a few suggestions, and they picked a superhero movie that neither had seen. He set the projection up for them and then left them to it. The sound and picture quality were outstanding, not that Ras would have expected anything less.

The movie played on, explosions and superhuman feats performed on the screen. Yet his mind was a million miles away. He was daydreaming, on the palace balcony where his family had always addressed the citizens. He saw himself wearing the crown, standing next to his bride. He was formally introducing her to the island's people, her face shielded by the brim of a large black hat.

The population of Ko Pha Lano was clapping and cheering loudly, yelling out welcomes and hurrahs. His subjects looked optimistic, like they had when Queen Sirind used to address the crowd. In turn, Ras was overcome with joy and with hope that his reign would be a good one for the citizens he had the great privilege to serve. In the vision, he put his arm around his bride's shoulders. He was in love, the enrapturing, all-consuming force he'd imagined it to be. He remembered seeing it in his parents and knowing what it was. So grateful to have it for himself, he nodded to his father who sat off to the side, smiling at the young couple. Ras turned his beloved so that she could better see the people and they her, because her face was obscured by that hat.

When he did, the blond waves of her hair caught the light and her beautiful face emerged like a mirage. Only, it was not Vajhana beside him, ready to lead as queen. No, it was Gracie. It was Gracie the people were admiring and approving. The ovation was for her. Ras had to close his eyes for a minute to take in the sublime perfection of his hallucination. It was the best he'd ever had.

Then his mind ricocheted, wishing to but suddenly unable to re-create the pure bliss of his waking dream. Contentment in the present moment was all he had. Following that theory, he decided on their next activity. When the film ended, he summoned Gracie. "Come with me."

"Where are we going?"

"It's a surprise." He led her down the corridor, everything dark on board save for some safety lighting. Silence allowed only the sound of the ocean, fierce in its turbulence. He led them to the spa, where they'd shared their first kisses. What they hadn't shared was that magnificent rain forest shower. An omission that had tantalized him ever since and was about to be remedied.

The one night-light provided a silver glow. He swept his arms around Gracie's waist and under the loose blouse she was wearing. Lifting it right over her head in one fluid motion, he tossed it to a nearby chair. "I've been wanting you naked for hours," he rasped and with that, eased her pants down and helped her step out of them until he got his wish. The shadows played against her skin, creating light patches and dark stretches, all a gorgeous work of art that aroused him to the point that he had to rid himself of his own clothes as well.

Taking her into the shower, he positioned her under one of the heads so that he could get all of her hair wet, working with purpose as he ran his hands through the locks, taking one break for a long, hot, needy kiss. He ran his palms everywhere, from her breasts to the small of her back to between her legs and groaned when he felt her press her sex into his cupped hand. He held it steady and let her set the tempo that was right, stroking her until she came apart, making him the luckiest man on earth. He wrapped his arms around her and held her close until she settled down, although he was far from done.

With water jets spraying them from every angle, he backed her against one of the shower walls and pressed himself tight to her. "I want you so much, Gracie."

"Mmm…" Her seductive meow egged him further, until he maneuvered them so that he could lift one of her legs, giving him leverage to enter her with a pendulous swoop. Her cry of excitement echoed. He took her slow but solidly, his body deciding for them as his passion was urgent. Again they joined in the new dance they'd created together. Ras wanted it to go on forever although, eventually, their bodies reached a height, a summit, a peak where they slipped into free-fall together, holding each other for stability.

Once they found their footing again, they kissed gently, lovingly. Ras used the strawberry-scented shampoo to wash Gracie's hair, wanting to see the suds he created and then watch them cascade down her shoulders when he used a handheld showerhead. Then, in turn, she lathered his body with a soap that had a refreshing citrus aroma. Such power did she have over his reaction that he became stiff again. He sat down on the stone bench inside the shower and pulled her onto his lap. He couldn't have this woman on his continent, in his palace bedroom, by his side on the royal balcony. But this he could have, this he could allow himself. Although an ache in the center of his being told him loud and clear that he was in danger. What he felt for her went far past carnal. And had maybe become something he wasn't going to be able to live without.

Many hours later a pink and dewy Gracie rolled over toward him from underneath the pearly gray sheets. "Good morning?"

"I don't think so." His fingers instinctively

brushed aside a few strands of hair that were in her face. "We've slept well into the afternoon."

"Well, it was our sea day, anyway."

"After all, we were up so late."

"I'm glad we got a chance to visit the spa again."

"Maybe today I should give you a massage." She shot a smile into his heart.

He called an order in to David. Meeting him at the door, Ras carried the tray to the bedside. They ate leisurely, occasionally popping something into the other's mouth. Afterward, they sat by the pool, taking a swim here and there.

"Okay, we're going to avoid places like the White House and the Pentagon when we get to DC."

"More than that, Gracie. I don't want to be anywhere near Dupont Circle where a lot of the embassies are. There are a lot of danger zones in that city."

"How about the Smithsonian museums?"

"Better not."

"What were you planning to do when you visited?"

"I hadn't decided that I was going to. Remember, I had no itinerary until I met you. My only agenda was to have none."

"Hmm, let's see… I'm assuming a dashing prince such as yourself is an airplane pilot."

"At your service."

She picked up his phone. "I'm making reservations. Take me flying."

CHAPTER EIGHT

RAS APPROVED AS they were shown to the plane
Gracie had rented them outside the no-fly zones
of the nation's capital. Helping her into the cockpit, he surveyed the appointments, such as the
sleek leather seats and modern design. "Nice
details. Good research." After she was comfortably seated, he swooped in for a kiss on her
cheek.

Gracie didn't know the first thing about air-
planes but when she was scrolling through the
options, she went for the well-reviewed and the
best money could buy. That's how Ras seemed
to like it, and why would she argue?

"Ready for takeoff?" he asked as he settled
himself beside her in the two-seater, single-
engine plane. The crew had pulled it out of the
hangar so all that was left was for Ras to fly
away. He performed some safety checks and
radio communications to the controller, all ef-

fortlessly as if he flew a plane every day. Fortunately, he held pilot licenses in many countries including the US. "Here we go."

He soared them into the air as if they were a great winged bird, taking them up higher and higher. "This is wonderful."

"It's a great feeling, that's for sure." Once he was at a leveling altitude, he used one hand to reach over and squeeze her knee in a gesture of togetherness before returning it to the controls. This was another marvelous escapade they were on together. She quivered thinking about all they'd been occupied with for the past few days. Missions such as finding creative activities to do in a shower. Proving that nighttime might be used for pursuits other than sleeping. And so on. Even though it made no sense, and what happened in the Atlantic Ocean was going to stay in the Atlantic Ocean, they had been writing poetry together, with their bodies and with their souls. Making an unexpected meeting in the middle that had her concocting forbidden fantasies.

Everything about Ras had jolted her into realizing that her proclamations about spending the rest of her life alone were based on misinformation. Her parents and Davis had been her education in human relations, and they weren't good teachers. In fact, the instruction she'd received from them was terrible. She'd never understood the deep well-being of feeling supported and cheered on. The empathy and compassion and sincere concern she and Ras had for each other wasn't to be found in that incomplete guidebook she'd been handed. The world with him was as new as the open skies in front of her. Or maybe it was just the fresh lens she now saw it through. She'd never be the same after him. And feared that she couldn't bear there to even be an *after him*. Yet she knew the rules so she breathed in to take it for all it was worth, gliding through the skies.

"Take the controls," Ras said after a while.

"What?"

"You do it. You fly the plane."

Shock widened her eyes. "Ras, I don't know how to operate a plane."

"I'll talk you through it. Take hold of the yoke." He pointed to the U-shaped handle that was twin to the one he was using to maneuver their flight.

"I can't. You don't want to die, do you?"

His laughter bounced around the cockpit.

"We're not going to die. I'll manage our speed. You'll be in charge of altitude. The yoke is your means of going up and down. Get it together, Gracie baby, because you're about to cross the sky."

"Wh-what?" With hands that were shaking, she put both where he showed her. Her heart pounded a million times a minute. He had to be joking, letting her pilot the plane. But she sure as heck wanted to do it, wanted to feel the power to keep this mechanical bird in the sky. Nerves were fine as long as she concentrated. He knew what he was doing.

"Pull back on the yoke to nose up, push it forward to slant down. Here we go," he said as he flipped a couple of switches. "You're in the hot seat now."

At first, all she could do was try to keep steady, too afraid to make any moves, every muscle in her body tense as stone. "Oh, great, no big deal. Are you saying I have our lives in my hands?"

"No, ultimately I do. Your job would be to keep us from crashing into other planes, tall mountains, that type of thing."

She gritted her teeth and steeled her eyes. "Ooh!" she cried out.

"Okay, now, do something. I'll keep my eyes trained for any notification. We should be fine. Take her down a little bit."

"Are you kidding?"

"How else would you get the hang of it?"

"Ah! Here we go." She pushed forward on the yoke, which moved the nose of the plane slightly downward.

"Now level it out."

"Am I doing it right?"

"Good." She then reversed the motion, pulling back on the yoke to raise the nose upward. "Atta girl."

"This is great." Gracie had to admit it was exhilarating, all that ability in her hands. Soaring through the sky. Until she accidentally pushed the yoke too far forward and the nose began heading down at an unsafe angle.

"Gracie!" she heard Ras's voice tell her, "Gracie, pull up."

All of a sudden she got confused. Her heart raced.

"Ras?"

"Pull up!"

She summoned all of her focus and yanked back on the yoke until they reached a level position.

After they were stable he asked, "What happened?"

"I don't know. I froze."

"You recovered beautifully, and that's what matters most." She blew out a breath and acknowledged his encouragement. "Keep going."

When it was time to land, Ras resumed control of the plane. What an amazing thrill that had been, the one bobble notwithstanding. She'd surely never pictured even being in a two-seater. And she loved that Ras was confident enough in her to let her give flying it a try. After they deplaned and walked toward the hangar he asked, "Would you try it again sometime? You did great."

"Good heavens, yes. It was so much fun."

"Everything with you is fun."

She reached in her purse for her sunglasses and slipped them on, feeling cool and glamorous with the handsome prince by her side.

"Welcome to The Rosecrans." A valet took the fob for the Porsche from Ras so they could enter the fine-dining restaurant Gracie had chosen in Washington, DC, after they'd agreed that a lunch in town wouldn't result in too much visibility. Although as soon as he'd stepped out of the car and observed the comings and goings on the steps and under the welcome veranda, he was uncomfortable. Seeing people in traditional dress from every corner of the world mingling with business people in suits and women in designer fashions and elaborate jewelry, he felt noticeable. Just as he'd remembered, everywhere in Washington, DC, seemed to be teeming with visitors in town for official functions, conferences, meetings, benefits and so on. There was no avoiding the international melting pot, which was wonderful on the occasions when that had been his purpose here. Now, as a stop on his *time off* from being His Royal Highness, he didn't want to belong.

He cast his eyes downward, a move Gracie noticed right away. "Is this not to your liking?"

"I'm sure it's wonderful, just the type of place a crown prince would eat."

"Oh. Shall I find us somewhere else?"

"This is how Washington is. It's probably fine. Just a shock after our morning in the skies." What an enjoyable time he'd had high above it all with Gracie. He'd loved showing her a bit about how to pilot and watch her attempt it. Even if she was afraid, as he suspected she was, she still charged forward with all of her might. She never ceased to fascinate him. In fact, he was quite sure she never would. Not that he would have that chance to experience life with her.

When they entered and approached the reception podium, Ras immediately noticed the facial features and name badge of the hostess as being Thai. While his island was a sovereign nation in the gulf, he was naturally much more well-known in Thailand than anywhere else. She gave him a look, perhaps just acknowledging that they were both likely from the same part of the world. But what if she did recognize him as the prince? Would she mention it? To him or to anyone else? This was just what he was hoping to avoid. Being seen far from home with an unknown woman, especially given that his fiancée's entertainments were already being well documented.

Nonetheless, he allowed the hostess to seat them as Gracie had wisely reserved a secluded booth in the back of the restaurant. The hostess walked away but then quickly returned, seemingly looking at something on her phone. She walked past their booth but the whole encounter made Ras very uneasy.

After they ordered Ras said, "I know our agreement was that you would choose our entire itinerary during our time together. But I'm just not comfortable here in Washington, so let's leave after lunch. At the reception desk, I felt like I'd met everyone I laid eyes on at a state dinner or some such. A person can easily get lost in New York. Not here."

"I'd been thinking that next we'd spend some

time in the Hamptons, and then finish up in New York City."

"I love that idea. Why don't we give up the yacht and rent a house there? We can cook and swim and find some other private pursuits."

"To adventure," she said, offering the toast with a wily smirk.

"Adventure." They clinked glasses and that sexy smile of hers tightened his belly in the most delightful way.

Arrangements were made. After eating, they returned to the yacht to gather their items and Neo drove them to a helipad. In the air, Gracie grabbed his hand and her palpable excitement transferred to him as they descended into Bridgehampton, Long Island, one of the cluster of beachfront towns where the rich and the famous escaped the bustle of New York and just about everywhere else in the world.

Ras had been brought out to Long Island by limo to attend parties and summits over the years but had never stayed long. The oceanfront mansion Gracie selected had access to a private bay for water activities. He'd asked her to find a very special property, and it appeared she'd heeded his request. Upon landing, they were met by the rental agent, Miranda, who walked them in through the entry foyer with wide open glass doors and marble floors. "You have eight thousand square feet of living space." Ras had no idea what they'd do with that much house although every square foot meant that much more seclusion. He was already letting out sighs of relief from leaving Washington as quickly as possible.

"What a kitchen," Gracie remarked as Miranda led them farther into the mansion. "The granite countertops blend into the white cabinetry, which gives it a kind of homey look."

"And this is just your front kitchen for poolside snacks or a breakfast on the terrace. You have a full catering kitchen in the back." As they followed Miranda for the grand tour, Gracie took in every detail. "Formal dining room comfortably seats twenty. You have a total of four fireplaces, three here on the first level and another in the master suite."

"Billiards room." Gracie leaned in to ask Ras, "Do you play?"

"Sure."

"We'll see about that. We Jersey girls know our way around a pool table." She winked at him, which might have set his heart on fire.

"Private office, top-of-the-line connectivity, of course," Miranda said, pointing. The next area she showed them was done in woods and dark greens, with leather furniture and lots of end tables. "That's your den and full bar, and the game room beyond."

She walked them through another set of double doors to the sunroom, completely enclosed in glass and open window screens with an unobstructed view of the ocean. The furniture was wrought iron, cushions in uplifting yellow and orange tones. Ras noted that there were no other buildings anywhere around them.

Miranda suggested they explore the outdoor amenities on their own, and took them up the grand central staircase in the foyer to the second level. She pointed out a couple of the guest rooms and brought them to the master suite.

"I love all the white!" Gracie exclaimed. The wraparound room featured a sitting area on one side and a gigantic bed with a white gauze canopy on the other. The same white gauze floated across every window, allowing breezes in and out, and a 180-degree view of the ocean and the rolling green lawn leading to the bay. A fireplace faced the bed.

"Double dressing rooms, a furnished terrace with rocking chairs, loungers and a breakfast table."

He indulged in a long gander of Gracie from the hair on her head to the sandals on her feet while she chatted with Miranda. This bedroom suite was so complete, he wondered why they'd even bother with any other part of the house.

Once they settled into the Hampton mansion, Ras was in a much better mood. It hadn't occurred to Gracie that even with a baseball hat, jeans, T-shirt and other manners of casual dress, he'd still feel exposed and not even want to visit museums and monuments. That was okay. Seeing the Hamptons on a best-of-everything basis was going to be great.

"Eight bedrooms. Is that what Miranda said?" she asked Ras as they unpacked. When the rental agent was here, she'd tried to get her mind off her goal to spend time with Ras in each and every one of them during the week they'd planned to stay.

"That's what she said," he replied, smiling. She watched him bend to reach for a case, the sinewy muscles of his back taut against his sky blue shirt. Oh, how she'd enjoyed reaching around him to hold those muscles when he was on top of her. "What are we going to do about food?"

"Miranda said the kitchen was well stocked, and she emailed me a list of local restaurants."

"Let's avoid restaurants as much as we can,

if that's okay. I just want to relax in this house while we're here."

"Do you want to go downstairs and visit the kitchen with me?"

"Absolutely."

They descended a second staircase that led to the back rooms of the house. "Oh, my goodness." Miranda wasn't kidding when she said the small front kitchen off the entrance was just for light fare. The main kitchen was not to be believed. A catering space ample for large parties, there was an island in the center at least four times larger than a typical kitchen would have. At one end of it sat four barstools for a casual cup of coffee or bite, positioned to face the wall-mounted television. "What beautiful choices with this custom cabinetry, countertops, floors, lighting. It's traditional but understated."

"It is finished in nice colors," he commented, regarding the tan paint with green glass accents.

Above the center of the island, a rack displayed at least two dozen pots and pans, and the perfect tools for whatever the task.

Gracie opened drawers and cabinet doors here and there, finding an amazing assortment of dishes, from those made of unbreakable materials for poolside to the finest china for the dining room. She slipped between two double doors and then called out to Ras. "You have to come see this."

She stood in a massive pantry. Shelves lined every bit of it, of varying heights dependent on what they were to hold. There were dry goods, canned foods, baking supplies.

"Do you like to cook?" Ras asked.

She liked being in the center of the pantry with him. While it was plenty big, it still gave her an intimate feeling. Like this food was theirs in their actual life today. Like this wasn't just a big fantasy that would come to a crashing end and leave her alone. Her plan had been to tour the New England B&Bs after this time with Ras. Alone, and homeless to boot, with the contents of the boxes she left at Jen's all she owned. Not even a shelf to store a can of tuna fish. That was what she had wanted. Most unexpectedly, things had changed and her decisions didn't entirely match what was now in her heart.

But for the moment, there was Ras. She looked into those welcoming eyes that always seemed to be seeing her through a complimentary lens. She could rest in his eyes for their time in this house; she could trust them. Why not give herself over fully to what had transpired between them? They both knew it wasn't forever. She could take that much risk. "I'd love to cook in a kitchen like this."

"What would you make?" He ran his fingertips from behind her ear down to the base of her neck, producing a shiver through her.

"Do you cook?" she moaned, her voice altered by the sensations racing through her body.

"As a matter of fact, I do on occasion. Naturally, the palace staff cringes when I enter their territory. But my mother taught me how to make a decent Pad Kra Pao, a meat stir-fry, and Som Tum spicy and sour salad."

"You're making my mouth water." She *might* have been referring to the description of the food.

"I'll cook them for you. We'll order the ingredients and have them delivered. But I still want to know what you're making me tonight."

"Let's look at what else is here. Where are the fresh foods?" Unsurprisingly, she found a second pantry containing more bins and baskets brimming with fruits and vegetables. The walk-in refrigerator was filled with perishable meats and cheeses. "What I was thinking of but am not seeing here are lobsters. Nearby Maine is where the most famous American lobsters come from."

"Order some. Have them delivered immediately."

"I'll call the grocery store in town that Miranda recommended. I'm sure they'll take care of it."

And sure enough, within two hours the doorbell rang. By the time she and Ras got from the back of the property where they were walking in the garden to the front door, the delivery truck was pulling away. What remained was a large cooler on wheels. Ras grabbed the handle and pulled it into the kitchen. When they flipped open the top, they were both startled at what they found inside. Four lobsters. Alive!

"Hello," Ras greeted them.

They both bent over to get a better look, and when one of the lobsters seemed to snap its claws at Gracie, she jumped back. "I didn't know I needed to clarify that we wanted them... well, you know...dead."

"At least we know they're fresh." One snapped its claws again to make the point, and Ras closed the top of the cooler. "For safekeeping. How were you planning to cook them?"

"I saw a big lobster pot. I assumed we'd just

steam them and have them with drawn butter. The classic American way."

"Carry on."

Gracie quickly looked up the recommended amount of water and salt to boil. When it was time to put the lobsters in, though, she was hesitant. "The instructions say headfirst."

"Are you ready for me to open the cooler?"

She swallowed hard. "I suppose it's now or never."

He flipped back the lid again. All four of the crustaceans were moving around. "Can you do it for me?" she pleaded.

"No, no, Miss Gracie," he teased. "You said you were going to cook for me."

"They just seem so…alive."

"That's usually the order of things, alive to dead to food. The other way around is a challenge."

"Come on, you own an island. I'm sure you're used to a lot of live fish and seafood."

"Yes, but I'm a prince. I don't have to kill it." He let out a belly laugh that gave her the giggles, too. "And I don't actually own the island."

"I can barely squash mosquitos that suck my blood in the summertime."

"I thought you said you Jersey girls were tough?" She rolled her eyes.

"I'm calling that little one Lucky," Ras continued. "That was my dog's name when I was growing up. My mother used to tell him how lucky he was to be in such a privileged family. I think she was teaching me a lesson about humility."

"Lucky? This Lucky is *lucky* to be in the company of two people who could just eat something from the pantry."

"Do you want soup?"

"I'm calling that shinier one Diamond."

CHAPTER NINE

WITH THEIR NEW friends Lucky, Diamond, Amphitrite and Hampton ensconced in the refrigerator for the night, Ras and Gracie went upstairs. They'd eaten the canned chowder and fresh bread with butter as they sat on the stools at the kitchen island watching a baseball game on TV. Ras loved the simplicity. The topic of lobsters, with the help of the internet, added to the dinner entertainment.

"'Why do lobsters make lousy friends?'" she asked, reading from her phone.

"Why?"

"'Because they're shellfish.'"

His turn. "A lobster reported a crime to the police. They asked him to be more Pacific."

"Did you hear about the lobster who couldn't go to the gym because he pulled a mussel?"

"What do you call a lobster that's afraid of tight spaces?"

"I don't know," she said as he buttered two more thick slices of bread and put one on her plate and the other on his.

"*Claws*trophobic."

"What about one that's overworked?"

"Um…a…frustr*acean*."

"Ha. Very good."

They volleyed back and forth until they finished eating.

"How does a lobster answer the phone?" she asked, finishing her jokes.

"Shello?"

They put the dishes into one of the dishwashers. Miranda had let them know the housekeepers' schedules, which Ras memorized.

"Let's take some dessert and tea upstairs for later," she suggested, grabbing what she wanted and then stopping to open the refrigerator. "Good night, Lucky. Good night, Diamond. Good night, Amphitrite. Good night, Hampton. Have a chill rest."

"What are we going to do with them tomorrow?"

"Let the housekeeping staff enjoy them. I'm sure they'll be able to deal with it once they have their morning *claw*fee." With that, they shut the lights in the kitchen and went giggling upstairs.

Out the bedroom windows, the sky was a shimmering blue, the moon pearly as it cast beams onto the ocean. Even Ras, who'd been around the earth, had to take in the tranquil beauty of it all. Not to mention the beauty of the woman in the room, who he'd come to feel more natural with than without.

She lit the candles that had been thoughtfully placed throughout the suite, no doubt left by staff who acknowledged the romance of the setting. With that flickering orange of the flames surrounding them, Ras slipped off the sundress Gracie had on and all but gasped at the glow of her skin. With only undies beneath, he hastily slid them of. Quickly shedding his own clothes, he pulled her onto the bed. "You've changed my world, Gracie. I'll never be the same after this time we've spent together."

"I know," she replied gently, running her fingernails along his arm, shocking his body to attention. "I will always remember this."

"I don't want it to ever end."

"It has to, Ras. You have your duties to fulfill."

"Yes. My obligation above all else is to produce an heir, so that when my reign is done, the monarchy will continue."

"Even if you have to marry someone you wouldn't have chosen."

"You've shown me…" Ras cut himself off. He did not want to say aloud what he suspected was in his heart. He didn't want her to hear it. He didn't want to hear it, either. Because it was of no relevance anyway. She understood the situation exactly as it was. And if he had been an unattached man, royal or not, she would never have let things go this far. His very unavailability was what made this possible. She knew how to protect herself and so only allowed this because soon he'd fly to the other side of the planet and they'd never see each other again. For her as much as for himself, he'd bite back the words that he wanted to sing.

"You might be surprised about the heir, though. You could end up with a child to adore." Her hand went to her belly, a motion he hadn't seen her make in a while. He tapped a light kiss onto her shoulder.

"My parents adored me. I could see it in their eyes. They loved each other, and I was an extension, a product of that love. That made all the difference."

She measured what he said. "I would have thought that, too. But when I was pregnant…"

A lump formed in his throat that she had to

say *when I was pregnant* knowing there was no baby at the end of that reminiscence. "Continue."

"Even though Davis wasn't a good man and I never felt secure in my future with him, having a baby grow in my belly was the most amazing thing." Her voice took on a crackly tone he hadn't heard before. "Somehow, as soon as I found out I was pregnant, I envisioned that little being inside me. He, or she, I never did find out, was real to me. My blessing and my responsibility. It was truly awesome."

"I can't imagine how painful that loss must have been. Especially without a partner."

"It was almost as if the baby was my partner. Before that horrible day in the bus station bathroom when the stabbing pain told me it was over. It was like the baby and I were invincible. Together, we could do anything. Everything that my parents were, and weren't, didn't matter. I was going to set everything straight, right all the wrongs."

"You'll have the opportunity again if you want."

"I told you, no men, no babies. It's just me against the world now."

"If I had the chance to, I'd show you that wasn't how it had to be." He wrapped his arms

tightly around her, completely encircling her.
The way he wanted it. They way he'd always
want it. The way it would never be.

Gracie woke early and turned to admire Ras's
sculpted cheekbones and jaw in repose. Not
wanting to wake him, she slinked out of bed
and slipped on a pink silk robe, tying it at the
waist as she edged out of one of the double
doors onto the deck. Her bare feet padded the
wooden planks to reach the back staircase,
which she trotted down while admiring the
pale sunrise. Reaching the first floor, she went
straight for the kitchen. There she met Ini, the
kitchen manager.

"I'm Gracie. Did you get our note from last
night?"

"Yes, ma'am. I come in very early. The
groundskeeper removed the lobsters from the
refrigerator and brought them to my *grand-
mulita*'s house. We'll have a fine dinner, thank
you. Do you want coffee? I'll be happy to
make a tray before I leave and place it on the
table outside the master bedroom."

"That would be great."

Gracie stepped back outside, the early-
morning air moist and thick, feeling the cool-
ness under her shoeless feet. She went out to

the edge of the walkway that led to the bay. The dock had a small paddleboat, kayaks, even surfboards. She turned around to look at the mansion, and the open door on the upper deck helped her locate the master bedroom she'd just came out from. Where Ras was hopefully still resting in peaceful slumber.

Cinching the waist of her robe again, she absentmindedly caressed the lapel up and down, her finger mimicking one of the many kinds of touch Ras had bestowed on her. The way he had held her so tightly she thought he'd never let her go. The way she didn't want him to.

"What's going on down there?" Ras appeared on the deck. His hairless chest was bare. That she could see the tops of his pelvic bones above the deck's railing made her believe he was totally naked head to toe. He raked his long fingers through his hair.

"Just breathing in the morning. I didn't want to wake you."

"How kind of you."

His smile would give the noonday sun a run for its money.

The scene was idyllic. She could imagine it was real. That they were together, coupled, partnered, friends. All of which she'd have never dreamed of as a child. When she was brutally alone with a neglect that branded into her skin like a hot iron. Unwanted, cast aside, insignificant. When she was young, she thought she'd done something to deserve her parents' lack of interest in her. But by adolescence a steely instinct in her grew, telling her that she was a victim of circumstance. That it wasn't her fault. Although she'd always have that cross to bear.

She heard the sound of a truck backing out along the driveway that flanked the backyard. Ini was driving, with the groundskeeper in the passenger seat. They waved goodbye. Ini wasn't kidding that they really did work an early shift.

That left her alone with her own personal angel who'd been sent to her when she was making the gigantic changes in her life that had taken all of her wherewithal. The fates were so benevolent to send Ras to her. She was so, so grateful. Why were tears spilling down her face?

"There should be a tray with coffee right outside the bedroom door," she yelled up, wiping her eyes with the backs of her fingers.

"Are you coming up? Better yet, I'll bring it down. Let's sit outside."

She held her breath long enough to get the

drops to stop falling from her eyes and called, "That would be lovely."

Last night was the most she'd ever confided about the miscarriage. Sure, Jen had come to visit, and brought her sandwiches and extra blankets. But there hadn't been that much to say. The doctor explained that these things occurred with a prevalence higher than people realized, but that Gracie was young and healthy and there was no reason she couldn't start trying for another baby soon. The doctor, of course, not knowing that the father of the miscarried fetus was not around and not coming back into the picture. Sure, on occasion, she'd considered using a sperm donor or other alternative arrangements people made. But the ordeal was too much of a heartbreak to return from. Losing the baby was another desertion, and she was not going to take any more chances on that. She'd been left enough for a lifetime. Her edict was signed, sealed and delivered. Then she'd met Ras.

"Why are you crying?" Ras approached with both the tray and a worried look on his face. He'd pulled on a pair of pajama bottoms.

"No reason," she told him, brushing more tears away. Neither of them bought her false bravado.

"No one cries for no reason," he said as he put the tray down at a table and chairs by the pool. He wrapped her into his arms. The way he constantly hugged her like that was almost unbearable in its promise.

"I'm just happy, Ras. You've given me this amazing opportunity. And you've been so nice to me."

"Your parents and that horrible Davis were fools," he whispered into her ear. "I wish I could spend every day of the rest of our lives showing you how you should be treated."

She laid her face against his smooth chest and tried to compose herself, knowing that what he said could not come true and wondering how she was going to live without him.

While they had breakfast, he placed an order with a grocery store for the ingredients he needed for the Pad Kra Pao and Som Tum he'd promised to make her.

"I need green papaya, fish sauce, dried shrimp, long beans, palm sugar," he said, going over his list with the grocer. It being the Hamptons, a wide variety of gourmet and international foods were available for the asking so Ras was sure he'd get all the specific items he needed. That a queen had taught her son the crown prince to cook a few family favorite dishes tickled Gracie's heart. Not to mention the permanent taste of bitterness that her parents hadn't even provided her with food half of the time when she was growing up. "And you have the holy basil? It can't be sweet basil…oh, from a local grower? Fantastic!"

"All set?" she asked when he was finally done with the long list.

"Be prepared to be dazzled." He winked at her.

Without another word, he stood and slid off the pajama bottom he had on. And, in one fluid motion, dove naked headfirst into the deep end of the pool and swam across its considerable length before his head popped up on the other side. He shook out his hair and smoothed it back with two palms. "Join me."

It was a week of relaxation and bliss. He showed her how to use a mortar and pestle, and together they created those spicy and enticing dishes from his childhood that made her tongue tingle. From the house's extensive digital music library, she played him all of her favorite songs and they danced naked around the empty rooms of the mansion, arms outstretched like children. She beat him at billiards, and then they used the pool table for a different purpose. They also tested out all of the other beds in the house…for comfort. They went out on the water every day. One night they made a bonfire in the backyard pit and roasted marshmallows on long sticks. Feeding each other the gooey mess necessitated licking it from each other's fingers. They took long walks on the beach, so long, in fact, that sometimes they'd just collapse to rest a bit before continuing, lying on their backs in the pillowy dry sand, watching the sun come up or fade down. Ras felt safe. He left another voice mail for the king that he was fine and would see him soon.

Too quickly, the week was done. "So it's into New York City tomorrow," he said while stroking the hills and valleys of her body as they lay on a thick rug in front of one of the downstairs fireplaces.

"Yes, sir. I've chosen a hotel penthouse with a private entrance and elevator."

"The big city and the masses."

"Would you rather not go?"

"No. I'd love to see New York. With you."

"If it's okay with you, we'll go to the Met Museum and to a Broadway show, and I've got reservations for a trendy Scandinavian restaurant." His brows crossed. "What's wrong?"

"Only that it will be my last week with you.

You're the sight I most want to see. How will we say goodbye after next week?"

She gulped air. "What choice do we have?"

Bright lights, big town. The driver who had picked them up at the house in Bridgehampton now opened the door for them to exit at the side entrance to the five-star Manhattan hotel where their personal elevator awaited. Per the instructions they had received, she punched in a key code at a small gate and they gained entry. Inside the elevator there was only one button, labeled *P*, and up they shot to the sixty-fourth floor.

"This is even better than the photos on the website," Gracie stated. She was right, the penthouse was magnificent.

A master bedroom was partitioned off with half-walls that came from the center of the space like spokes in a wheel. From there, they passed through to the master bath, also partitioned off to create separate areas. Farther around the circle was a dressing area and relaxation room. Next came a full living and dining suite.

"You did good. I love it." With all the windows, it was like having a home on the observation deck of the Empire State Building.

From the green of Central Park to the north and the towers of Wall Street to the south, Ras was reminded that Manhattan was the start of his journey, meeting beautiful Gracie as the cruise ship made its way around the Statue of Liberty. Cuban coffee and sexy dancing in that Miami club, what an odyssey it had truly been. Though, on leaving his father at the UN he'd had no idea that it would turn out to be a voyage of the heart as well. One that would change him forever.

But there was still a glorious five days left. He turned to his tour guide to ask, "What are we doing first?"

"Tonight, we have a box at the opera." She moved through to the dressing room and opened the closet doors wide. A tuxedo and all of its accessories hung waiting. "I hope you don't mind, but I ordered this to be delivered. I took a guess at your size."

"You are a clever one. You are really getting the hang of this." He gave a full press of his lips to hers. Although he would be delighted to apply a half million additional kisses to her from head to toe, he refrained. "What will you be wearing?" he asked, remembering that she had some pretty dresses but nothing to wear to the opera.

Opening the closet on the other side of the room, a shimmery gown encrusted with crystals, sparkling shoes and a silky wrap were ready. "I also rented this, charged to you, of course." She grinned.

Carried by the strong emotions of *La Traviata*, they enjoyed a bottle of wine in their opera box. Once the performance ended, they stepped out into the night at the Lincoln Center and walked around the fountain. Gracie was resplendent in her iridescent gown. It really could have hardly been more glamorous. Befitting a prince with the love of his life. He internally cautioned himself to get that thought out of his mind. The longer he let it live, the harder it was going to be to forget it. Not that he ever would.

Then, suddenly, it started to rain so they ducked into their waiting limo. Back at the penthouse, Ras removed his jacket and tie and sat down on one of the couches. Gracie slipped out of her dress and into a robe to join him. He wanted to check his phone for the weather forecast to see if that might necessitate any changes to their itinerary tomorrow. Happy to read that the light rain was expected to pass by morning, on a whim he decided to check a news outlet for the weather in the Gulf of Thailand, something he hadn't done in over two weeks. While there had been heavy downpours, that wasn't the news that caught his eye.

At the bottom of the screen was the click button for the *People* section and right next to it, sure as day, was a photo of His Royal Highness Crown Prince Rasmayada of Ko Pha Lano and Gracie Russo holding hands.

His gut sank. "Oh, no."

"What is it?" Gracie moved over to sit right next to him and he showed her the photo. He clicked through, dreading what he might find.

"Ras, I'm so sorry." There were two more photos of them. One with his arm around her, one a closer shot of them smiling at each other like newlyweds. "These were taken at that restaurant in Washington."

"Remember that hostess who I thought looked at me suspiciously?"

"The one who showed us to our table."

"Then she passed by us again and she was on her phone. She was taking photos. Which she must have sold."

"I'd like to report her to the restaurant management."

"Sure. Although the damage has already been done."

"Disgusting."

He tapped into one then another of the gossip sites that concentrated on young royals and the photos had made their way everywhere, just as he knew they would.

His Royal Highness is having quite a bachelor's last hurrah before marriage.

Ko Pha Lano's crown prince doesn't have eyes only for his princess.

And on it went.

Equally awful were new photos of Vajhana with her British earl. The gossip hounds didn't miss anything. Aboard a boat on the Seine with the glistening night lights of the Eiffel Tower behind them, the princess with a designer coat falling off her. "She and I deserve each other. We are royal embarrassments."

He stared out to the New York skyline, feeling Gracie's warm body beside him. Now he questioned the wisdom of this whole trip. He'd gained what his mother had wanted him to, but he'd taken it too far. She'd wanted him to explore himself. In the process, his spirit was set free. And it had found Gracie. His heart had discovered a reason to beat. It had learned the most fundamental emotion a human could have. Which would hurt much worse than never knowing love at all.

CHAPTER TEN

THE PARTY WAS OVER. It had been going to end anyway. Yet Gracie wished it was on its own terms, not having it decided for them by some restaurant hostess with no ethics. "We knew we were doomed, Ras. Fortune put us together to bolster us to walk our own paths." Her spin didn't even sound convincing to her, so she was sure it wouldn't to Ras, either. Still, she pressed on. "We still have a few more days. We can make the most of it." Yet she knew she wouldn't. Couldn't. Everything had been spoiled.

"You're right," he uttered in a low voice that was just as unconvincing. It was late but they still sat on the penthouse couch, overlooking the magnificence of New York. They were as physically close as could be; she could feel his body next to hers from shoulder to ankle. "The most of it…" he echoed, but trailed off.

For all of the constant conversation they'd

had, there was suddenly nothing to say. Eventually, they got up and went to bed. Lying naked, her in his arms, they didn't engage in the celestial lovemaking that had shown them both pleasures sent from heaven. They held each other nonetheless, not wanting to let go any sooner than they had to. She woke up alone in the gray of morning. She found Ras at the dining room table, drinking coffee on hotel china that was poured from a silver pot he'd no doubt had delivered.

"I couldn't think of what to order for breakfast. Can you take care of it?"

"Of course," she replied with a squeeze to his shoulder. She poured a coffee and sat down opposite him.

"I'm sorry you and I, what we shared, has to end with a taint," he said as if he'd been pondering it. "With a bad taste in my mouth. Someday I'll wear the crown, I'll produce the heir and carry on the legacy. But my record is marred. There will always be this as a footnote, showing me to have been reckless and impulsive. And you're not a footnote, Gracie."

"It wasn't wrong for you to have followed your instincts."

"I've let my people down. I've let my father down."

"Ras, your mother wanted…"

"I don't think she would have wanted this."

"I don't think she would have wanted you to marry someone you didn't love. Not from what you've told me of her."

He almost angrily snapped a retort but pulled it back and pierced her with his gaze. And took a slow breath. "What now?" It seemed like a question loaded with layers.

There was only one she could address. "Let's go to a downtown deli for a ridiculously big breakfast and then see some Soho galleries."

The idea brought a crack to the corner of Ras's mouth. "Carry on regardless, is that right?"

"Or we could stay here and mope around the penthouse all day."

He stretched his hand across the table for hers. He brought it to his mouth and kissed it. "Oh, my Gracie, you are one of a kind."

After their bellies were bursting from breakfast, Gracie created a route through the streets of Soho for them to walk. Despite it not being a particularly bright morning, he wore sunglasses and was dressed in faded jeans and his black leather jacket. They roamed the blocks where artists carried large canvases into their studios and boutiques sold small-label fashions. She'd researched and picked out a couple of galleries to visit. They discussed the art as they strolled. Honestly, though, the solemnity covered them like the dark clouds above. The joy was gone. Only the inevitable remained.

That night they dressed nicely for their chef's table at one of New York's most talked about restaurants that served updated versions of traditional Scandinavian food. They were brought into a private dining room. Although the smoked, dried and pickled fishes and the savory dumplings were delicious, Ras and Gracie were deflated and there were lulls in the conversation as both stared absently around the silent room that almost felt like a prison. She understood most fully that this was how Ras lived, separated from much of the world; his life could indeed be very lonely without the right person to share it with.

He finally said, "I think I should just go home tomorrow."

Her eyes opened wide, and she willed back the tears that were threatening. "I see."

"The sooner I get back to Ko Pha Lano, the sooner I can be seen fulfilling my typical schedule. The more I do that, the more my prenuptial follies will fade into the background. Hopefully Vajhana's, too. And our people can begin focusing on the upcoming wedding, which always raises morale."

"Will it raise yours?"

"I will do what is expected of me. It shouldn't be such a great sacrifice."

Giving him up would be a great sacrifice to her. He was right, though; he was born to rule over his people and that's what he'd do. Emotions had no part in the equation. Which did nothing to silence the thudding in Gracie's gut.

She scrapped their plans to go to a jazz club after dinner as neither of them was in the mood. In fact, Ras wanted to go back to the hotel and make arrangements for a private plane to fly him back to the island the next day. She began packing her things, as she'd be leaving as well if he wasn't going to be sharing the penthouse with her.

He offered to fly her anywhere she wanted, but her next destination was already set. After touching base at Jen's apartment, she'd go forward with her plans to rent a car and learn about New England B&Bs, where she'd be able to acquire complimentary nights from the owners. How gorgeous the changing leaves of autumn would have been, seen with her arm through Ras's, but that was never on the books and nothing had changed on that score. She tossed and turned in bed, not even able to relish her last night with this man who had rocked her world. Her stomach hurt. Perhaps the salted fish had been too strong.

In the morning, a car was waiting for them and they left the hotel as invisibly as they had come in. Ras had booked a plane at a private airport and asked her to see him off, after which the car would take her to Jen's. They laced fingers in the back seat, where she tried to memorize the feel of those big square hands that would never touch her again.

"What was your favorite place that we visited?" she decided to ask, even though chitchat wasn't going to ease the pain that saying goodbye was going to bring. "Did you see what you wanted to?"

"Gracie," he answered quietly, "what difference does any of that make? I met you. I got to spend this time with you that was far more important than a monument or a tourist attraction."

Once they arrived at the airport, a crew member took Ras's bags and they walked out onto the runway where his plane was waiting. The boarding staircase had been lowered and stood waiting for its one and only passenger. It was almost unbearable to look at. Each stair would take him farther and farther away from her.

They kissed passionately. Her hands slowly traversed up his back until she could wrap them around his neck. They hugged for dear life. Tears streamed down her face, uncontrollable. They held each other so tightly that the world disappeared. Until they were frozen in time, no airport, no island on the other side of the world. Only him. Only for one last moment.

Finally, it was he who broke the hold and took her by the shoulders. "This is it."

"I know."

"I'll think of you every day of my life."

"And I will you. Remember the things your mother told you. Stay human, stay grounded, stay loving."

"Goodbye, Gracie."

"Goodbye, Your Royal Highness."

With that, he pivoted and headed toward the plane. He had to. A minute longer and he never would. He was off to do what was right. She watched him ascend every step, each one stabbing her deeper as she knew it would. When he reached the top, he turned to give one last wave. Then he ducked his head to step into the plane, the last she would ever see of the most magnificent man on earth.

* * *

Ras kept his eyes on the window as the plane ascended to the skies. He didn't move his watch point until the clouds obscured the skyscrapers of New York, turning the past weeks into a puffy hallucination. The cruise. Miami. Savannah. Charleston. DC. Bridgehampton. And then New York. Had that all actually happened or had it been one long fantasy? Had Gracie really happened?

He sucked in an inordinate amount of air as he finally faced front in his seat. Upon boarding, he'd hardly noticed the amenities on the plane. There was a bedroom and full bathroom so that he could sleep and shower. A crew dedicated to his every comfort. Which began with an attendant placing a tray on the side table next to his seat. It contained everything from a wet washcloth for his face to a plate of finger food to a cappuccino, and a card spotlighting movies and podcasts he might find diverting during the flight. All very well intentioned although he stared at it blankly with no interest. The only thing he cared about was what he had left behind.

He instructed himself to take another set of measured breaths. And, with each exhalation, to let out what was to now become his distant past. To release it into the world as simply positive energy that should find its way to someone who needed it next. Because he had no use for it anymore. He reclined his chair into a chaise and breathed himself into a nap. When he woke, he was grateful that a couple of hours had passed. Since he was headed away from the person his heart had come to define as the very definition of home, he just wanted to get back to the island as soon as possible.

In fact, he opened his tablet on which he'd downloaded a prospectus from a manufacturing company that his father and King Yodfa were considering. He did an internet search to look into published reports on what effect similar industries had on the environment, and it was as he thought. Depletion of natural resources and polluted waters were hard to avoid without expenses so prohibitive they left no profit. Ras still didn't think this was the best direction to go in to bring more employment and prosperity to the islands.

He was going to confront his father to strongly disapprove of these proposals. While he wouldn't be king for hopefully several decades of his father's good health, he would assert his beliefs and not let them fall on deaf ears. He reviewed the proposals he himself had been compiling, large-scale marine conservation and ecotourism. A smile crossed his face. Gracie knew a lot about ecotourism and conservation. He'd forever be inspired by her ambitions, her wherewithal to overcome all she'd faced. In spirit, across the miles but soul to soul, he'd always be proud of her. And he'd want her to be proud of him.

"Oh, you're back," King Maho said with a bite of sarcasm as Ras marched through the central hall of the palace toward his quarters.

"I am, Your Majesty." He stopped in front of his father and bowed his head. Then, like it or not, he gave his father a hug. His absence had not been meant to hurt the king. He was genuinely sorry if it did. "Had you been following my whereabouts?"

The king resisted his son's embrace at first, perhaps to punish him. Ras's insistence finally resulted in a brief hug with a pat on the back from his father who answered, "One of our people saw you board the cruise ship, I received your voice mails, and left it at that."

"I appreciate you not pulling me away from my trip." Away from Gracie.

"No matter, though, as I was kept regularly informed along with the public that you and your fiancée have been traipsing halfway across the world with other companions. I hope the two of you can get your prenuptial restlessness out of the way so that the wedding can proceed as planned."

"I'm sorry to have been a worry. You remember what my mother said..."

"Yes, son, I remember everything about your mother." The great man paused as remembrances softened his expression. Which he then caught and corrected. "Fine, you've had your ramble. You're to enter into a mutually advantageous marriage in a few weeks. There's much work to do for our subjects, our primary purpose. I'll expect no further...distractions."

"About our guardianship of the island, Father." He looked the king in the eye. This wasn't easy. His father had suffered so much. But as a result, he'd lost touch. He was probably unable to absorb that many peoples of the world were unwilling to see economic growth as a justification for doing harm to the earth. His father and King Yodfa had old ideas that didn't fit with what was important to the new generation. "I read the final prospectus for the partnership with King Yodfa. And I don't like it."

"I don't believe you are to be king any time

soon, and while I sit on the throne we shall do things my way."

"Do you hear yourself, Father? Single-minded, not at all willing to acknowledge another's point of view?" He'd become both hardheaded and hard-hearted. Ras understood, more than ever. The man had lost the love of his life, the only woman who had ever meant anything to him. After that, days and nights had just become an existence. He had no enthusiasm for new ideas or to achieve great things. The vigor had been drained from him.

With his lips pressed into a thin line, Ras silently promised Gracie that he wouldn't let that become his fate, too. He owed it to her not to shut down.

"You must be tired from your...pleasure trip, Ras. Get settled back in. I'm sure your good senses will return."

"Oh, believe me, my..." Ras stopped himself. He had taken a very long way home. His father was right about that. Ras had to think of a different way to broach conflicts with the king. "If you'll excuse me, Your Majesty. Princess Vajhana is coming. I thought she and I would have a private dinner on the terrace."

"Very good. I'm sure the two of you have a lot to talk about."

After attending to the paperwork that had been stacked on his desk while he was away, he met Vajhana on the helipad at the castle. "Ras, *daahling*."

Yes, she really did use that exaggerated tone of voice like she was a movie star from olden times. She tripped a little bit on her high-heeled shoes and grabbed his arm. He reached to steady her, having forgotten how bony she was. He'd gotten used to Gracie's ripe and pliable body.

"Let's relax with a glass of white. I brought my tablet with so many wedding decisions to make."

Ras snarled a bit at the prospect of discussing whether pale peach or pastel orange roses would make better centerpieces at the reception. Didn't anyone understand that the wedding day was just an expense of money and pomp? What counted was a life together, the day in, and day out of how people treated each other and viewed themselves. One person understood that. And it wasn't Vajhana.

After he'd helped pick out as many songs for the band to play as he could, he adjusted his chair so that he was close and eye to eye to his intended. "Princess, I want you to listen to me. I did not appreciate one bit seeing photos of you carousing with that British earl. It was unseemly and beneath both of us."

"I could say the same about you. I was actually kind of surprised, Ras, when my cousin sent me those photos from Washington. You usually keep under the radar, don't you?"

"Yes, that was a horrible misjudgment." The photos, that was. He would never in a million years describe Gracie as a misjudgment. Quite the opposite. "I won't do it again. Can you say the same?"

This was the woman he was going to spend his forever with. They had to establish better ground rules for their relationship. "We still have our old agreement, don't we, Ras? About how we're going to survive being matched up by our fathers with no say in the matter."

"Behind closed doors. Not on the lap of an earl. Can we agree to that?"

"I'll try." This couldn't be easy for Vajhana. She hadn't asked for any of this, either. They barely knew each other past the superficial. Perhaps deep in her heart she was also lamenting that she'd never have a chance to fall in love.

"We're to have children. We must appear as a family." His jaw clenched.

Oh, Mother, he called out in his mind. *I want*

*a marriage like yours. I want to love like you
did. A love that made you and Father both
better people. Better parents. Better leaders. I
won't have that with Vajhana. Who am I serving in this lie? Who is this best for?*

"Jen, thanks again for letting me crash here
these past couple of days," Gracie said, coming
out of the bathroom while toweling her wet hair.
Her friend was eating a piece of toast at the tiny
two-person kitchen table wedged between the
refrigerator and the sofa where Gracie had been
sleeping. It was a compact apartment as far as
could be from the penthouse where she'd been
living that *other* life. The one that had died on
a private airport runway days ago.

"You're heading out today?"

"Yup. I pick up the rental car in Midtown,
and my first B&B is in Massachusetts."

"The autumn leaves are going to be gorgeous. Why do you look so gray?"

Gracie laughed. "I look gray?"

"You know, pale. Is it because of that guy?"
Gracie hadn't felt it right to give out Ras's identity, so she'd only told Jen that she'd met a man
on the cruise and they'd ended up doing some
additional traveling together on his yacht and
in the Hamptons.

"My stomach has been funny. Must be something I'm eating." After getting ready, she grabbed her two travel bags packed and ready by the door.

"Have some toast before you go."

"I want to hit the road."

"Okay, take a piece with you."

Gracie nodded and took the toast and a bottle of water. "Thanks again for continuing to keep my four boxes. They're really all I've got now." She had that roiling in her belly again that brought her hand to hold her stomach. She'd broken herself of the habit of doing that whenever memories of the past were conjured up. There was no reason to start again. She gave Jen a hug and headed out the door with the very real feeling that more changes were to come.

Driving out of the city was great. Obviously, she couldn't snub being driven in limos and town cars, but there was something to be said for getting behind the wheel herself. She spent the drive to her first destination absolutely *not* wondering what a handsome prince nine thousand miles away was doing. *Not* remembering what his embrace felt like. *Not* recalling the luminescence in his big eyes when he looked at her. Definitely *not* replaying the rumble of his robust laughter that echoed through the wide-open rooms in a Bridgehampton mansion. In fact, she so *didn't* hear the sound of his voice saying her name that she cranked up some loud music to keep her company as she careered down the highway.

"This building is a hundred and fifty years old," the owner of the Beaves Inn located in the Berkshire Mountains told Gracie as she gave her a tour. "As you can see, we've kept the Victorian decor in all the rooms. Yours is one of our most requested rooms, ultrafeminine, with cream, peach and sea green as our inspiration colors. Guests love it."

"I can see why. The white iron bedframe. The fireplace." Would Ras have liked this? His tastes tended toward the modern. Gracie smiled at the older woman who was rightly so proud of her property.

"Will you be joining us for dinner? We serve a three-course meal with two menu options for an additional charge. If not, I can direct you to half a dozen local restaurants."

Dinner didn't sound too good. She'd forced herself to finish the toast that Jen had given her in New York. Maybe sinking into that claw-foot bathtub would soothe her tummy ache. "No, but, thank you so much."

"I'll let you get unpacked."

"Thank you."

A while later, after deciding against the bath for fear of nausea, Gracie chose to go for a walk. The air was crisp and, indeed, the fall foliage was just as spectacular as it had been touted. The leaves in almost psychedelic hues of red, gold and orange were like observing art. In fact, that's what they were. Nature's art.

She wished that she could be sharing the moment with Ras. She wished that she could share any moment with him. As she walked the dirt path, the sun's rays casting shards of light against the flora, she felt at one with the world. Connected, part of something. Even though she was alone, she was the opposite of lonely. Because she had started living. She'd done it. She'd evolved into the next version of herself. Her truth blossomed like a seedling that finally had enough light and water to grow. It was Ras who had tended her garden. He was the nour ishment she'd needed. He'd given her something she'd never had before. Love.

Love.

Not a word she'd ever thought was going to pertain to her. It was a word she didn't have faith in. Because love might lead to hope. And, in her experience, hope always led to disappointment. The child who waited by the window for the parents who didn't come home at night. Or the young woman who hid in the bathroom until she heard the man she'd come to dread walking out the front door. No, hope wasn't supposed to be included in her marching orders. She was going to exist on sheer self-sufficiency and determination.

Why did the fates have a different idea? It was the cruelest of jokes they'd played to make her fall in love with a man who could never be hers. *Fall in love.* Yup, there was no other way to describe it. She'd tumbled head over heels in love with His Royal Highness Crown Prince Rasmayada of Ko Pha Lano. Her heart clenched and then that swell in her belly did, too. She loved him. With all of her heart and soul and every cell in her being. Tears streamed out of her eyes as she trekked, fallen leaves crunching under her feet. She cried because now she had more to tote. The burdens of her past would have to make room so that she could keep the love she had for Ras close for the rest of her life. A job she'd accept willingly. Her recollections of moments with him were the best possessions she had. She'd cherish them forever.

Gracie spent the next days touring New England, taking in breathtaking displays of color.

She stayed in a room that had a mahogany sleigh bed and another with a built-in window seat. She went for a bike ride and came across a covered bridge. She'd never seen one before. It was agonizing not being able to show it to Ras, but she convinced herself that she was in some way. That he was with her wherever she went.

One day toward the end of her travels around the area, she was walking around a gentle lake, the reflections of the trees and leaves mirrored on the surface of the still water. Nausea rolled through her insides, and she ran quickly to a trash receptacle to vomit. The sensations in her body that she'd been denying had been increasing. She did some mental math and couldn't ignore the solution to her equation.

The rain forest shower on the yacht. Making love under the jets of the water. They hadn't thought to bring condoms in with them.

Later, she asked the innkeeper to direct her to the nearest pharmacy. After the short drive and once back in her room with its claret-painted walls and Italian mosaic-tiled floors, she performed a very modern test. Its answer came as no surprise. It was more than merely memories of Ras she was carrying.

CHAPTER ELEVEN

RAS PACED HIS QUARTERS, looking out from the cliff where his rooms stood. He thought he might pace until his shoes were worn to shreds, letting the wind whoosh in from his windows as he trod back and forth, back and forth. His discontent left him tired in the daytime and wide-awake in the wee hours. His daily schedule was met without gusto. He was unhappy with every conversation he'd had with his father since returning to the palace. And despite his intentions when he got on that plane to come home after his voyage, he wasn't able to put it behind him. Quite the opposite. All he did was think about the trip. Not about the Spanish moss in Savannah or the lobsters in the Hamptons. *Her.* He couldn't stop thinking about *her.* The woman who had transformed the universe as he knew it. A world he couldn't seem to fit back into. Plain and simple, there was no ground without her. Without Gracie.

His lack of kilter was especially worse when he was with his fiancée, which was quite a sorry state of affairs. Vajhana could hardly seem sillier to him, a spoiled real-life princess who didn't care about anything but herself. With no interest in building a working pact with him or in the future of their nations. He found it hard to conceive of her being a good mother, either, when the time came. It wasn't her fault. She didn't really want this marriage, either. It also wasn't her fault that she wasn't the woman he was in love with.

He stopped moving long enough to stare out past the palace grounds. Arms crossed, a stance with legs apart, tension stiffened his body. Nothing would ever be right without Gracie. Nothing ever could. He needed to reunite with her, to profess his love in case she hadn't guessed how he felt. To beg her to be his forevermore. At any cost. Yet the reality of that need produced almost insurmountable obstacles. To call off the wedding to Vajhana would be to disobey not one but two kings. Gracie was a commoner. An American. No ties to the region whatsoever. At least his mother had come from a family of standing on the island. Gracie didn't even know the whereabouts of her parents. It was almost impossible.

He retrieved the little Gullah basket they'd bought in Charleston that he now kept on his desk by day and beside his bed at night. He ran his thumb along the tight weave of the grass. Although it was a small item it was solid, sturdy, enduring. He'd told Gracie to hold his kisses in hers.

Almost impossible. *Almost.* Why, he thought as he returned to his pacing while holding the basket in his fingers, shouldn't he have the love of his life? It would transform him into a stronger man. More importantly was the opposite concern. That he didn't know what would become of him if he didn't have the woman who made him whole at his side. He'd be beaten down. Embittered. His insides would turn to ash like his father's had. Preventing him from becoming the king he should be. He had to have Gracie back. Impossible. *Almost.*

"Your Majesty." He charged into his father's rooms after calling the king's personal secretary to make sure he was available. "I haven't told you everything about my time in the States."

He explained it all, from the Cuban coffees to the fact that the woman he was photographed with was not a vacation fling. That he was madly, desperately, eternally in love.

The king's response was anything but what

Ras had hoped. A decidedly inflexible, "Absolutely not," came roaring out of King Maho's mouth. "I told you this when you first returned home from your little carefree whirlwind. You have a duty to our people. That's the only calling you'll answer to."

Ras was unable to accept the answer, so strong were his feelings for Gracie. Why was his father entitled to love yet Ras wasn't? It was because the king had forgotten. Forgotten what life had been like until he'd buried a wife long before he should have. Forgotten the bond they'd shared, the joy, the closeness. The way any problem could be solved if they put their heads together. Forgotten the little smiles and the romantic gestures that made every day special. Or maybe it was that he remembered it all too well and was determined to protect his son from the heartbreak he'd faced.

King Maho's face changed as if he indeed was overcome by the sadness for what had been lost. His eyes opened into glassy circles like those of a child. But only for the briefest of moments. He stood up tall. "You and Vajhana will marry as agreed," he continued. "And that's the last I will hear of it."

In anger and defiance, Ras stormed out of the palace and off the grounds. He had to get away from the palace for a moment. The time in the US was successful in showing him that he could be a man among men, walking freely. Especially as no one expected to see him roaming through the streets alone. Although royal surveillance had followed him, they were in plain clothes and had the decency to stay a considerable distance behind.

Ras had to find a way to get through to his father, make him see what was best for the family. Once he met Gracie he'd be sure to like her; that kindness, so like Queen Sirind's, would be palpable to his father. They could make this work. Ras *had* to. Being with Gracie was life or death for him. Without her, he'd have no heart at all.

What if she wouldn't have him back? She was deeply into her New England tour now. As a matter of fact, it was coming to an end if his mental calendar served him right. Knowing her, she'd secured her next undertaking, which was to visit and rate the luxury accommodations in Boston. By now she'd probably booked clients into the places she'd visited with him, had probably made her first commissions and was off and running in her career. He couldn't bear to tear her away from something that was so important to her.

An idea struck him like a thunderbolt. It was a solution to a multitude of problems all at once. It was easily the best idea he'd ever had. Although there were many steps to take before it could be put into place.

Thoughts racing through his mind, he noticed two people walking their small dogs on leashes along the street, one going north and one south. When the dogs met they began circling and smelling each other, bouncing around each other at the thrill of a new acquaintance. One was a Yorkshire terrier and the other a Shih Tzu. Which of course reminded him of his childhood Shih Tzu, Lucky. How much fun Ras would have with his parents and Lucky, how happy his fa...

The second great idea of the day brought a mischievous smile to the prince's face. He pulled his phone from his pocket.

Later that day, he asked his father to meet him on the west lawn. That was an area on the grounds that had always been just for the family's use. The press was kept away, and no addresses or large functions took place there. As his father approached, Ras let go of what he hoped was going to be a messenger of détente. Who went running straight toward the king.

"What on earth is this?" King Maho shouted as he closed the gap between himself and Ras. The king bent down to pet the Shih Tzu who was jumping around him. The first dog in the palace since Lucky died.

"Remember Lucky, Father?"

"Of course I do."

"How he used to run around this lawn fetching sticks until he was panting with exhaustion."

"Yet always wanting to do it again," the king chuckled. Ras couldn't think of the last time he'd heard his father laugh. The king froze in place, looked into Ras's eyes and then shifted his gaze to the middle distance of the lawn, as if memories were flooding back to him.

"Remember those happy times, Father?" Ras pushed the point. "With mother so fun loving and caring? Her inner spirit touched everyone on our island."

"She loved everyone in the world, son," the king murmured in a soft voice.

"But no one more than you and I."

"Those were some…exceptional times."

"Gracie is like that, Father. She's the warmest person I've ever met besides mother. She's impossible not to love."

The dog was hopping onto the king's leg,

which prompted him to reach down and pick him up. As he began to pet him, the dog nuzzled his face against the king's chest. Without giving it a second thought, King Maho's fingers scratched under the dog's chin, a sensation that got a heavenly reaction.

"I think Mom's death took the best of you from us, Dad." He used the informal endearments he hadn't used in years. "I think the island could be a place of good cheer again. We can all mourn the loss of Queen Sirind for the rest of our lives yet still move forward with progress and pride. She'd want us to."

While in thought, the king didn't object when the dog squirmed up to kiss his face. Then, when he noticed, he shooed him off and the stern expression that had become his typical mask returned. And then he thought about something else. That made his eyes soften at the corners. A long, almost unbearable, pause followed.

He finally declared, "All right, son. Marry your Gracie. You deserve the happiness you are asking for."

Spontaneously, Ras hugged his father, the dog in the center of the embrace. The two men chuckled. Then Ras got back to business. "And I have some new proposals for you about the island. I assume when I break the engagement to Vajhana, King Yodfa will no longer be our partner."

"You'd better be darn sure of yourself then, Ras. You've got our whole nation depending on it."

"I am. I am." The dog gestured to be let down to the lawn. At which point he ran to explore every plant, every smell. The king and the prince stood side by side watching. "What shall we name him, Your Majesty?"

"We'll call him Lucky Two."

Gracie entered the Beacon Hill carriage house that had been converted into the lobby of an exclusive hotel in Boston. She had a spring in her step and was feeling well for a couple of reasons. One, the morning sickness that had been so torturous a few days ago had subsided a bit. Two, she'd booked a dozen clients for Carat Cruises' Nova Scotia voyage on *Liberation*, and would soon be receiving her commission. And three, today was the day she was going to tell His Royal Highness Rasmayada that she was pregnant with his child. She'd waited until she was away from the rural spots she'd visited in the New England countryside, where the bucolic serenity sometimes came with spotty phone and internet service. When she did reach him, she wanted to be sure he could hear her loud and clear.

After being shown to her room, she dipped her hand into her bag to retrieve her phone. Instead, she pulled out the little Gullah basket that she and Ras had bought in Charleston. He'd told her it would hold his kisses for her. She wasn't going to let it be a receptacle for her tears. Holding it in one hand, not letting go, she found her phone with the other.

She and Ras had had several conversations about Gracie's determination to no longer be tied down to anything that could disappoint her like her parents and Davis had. That she wouldn't even make one place her home. During one of the talks, Ras got very serious and punched a number into her phone. He'd told her she could forget about having it and that she never had to call. However, if she was ever in trouble, if she ever needed him, no matter how many years had gone by, she could always dial that number. He was going to be quite surprised to look down to his phone screen and see that she was calling him after such a short time. Sadly, he'd have to endure a moment of worry that she was taking him up on his offer because something was wrong. But she'd quickly inform him that she had gotten in touch for quite another reason.

After all, he needed to know about the miracle. That his child was growing in her belly. She touched her stomach like she had a million times before, only it was different now. As soon as she'd gotten to Boston, she'd seen a doctor and everything seemed to be fine. Of course, she could suffer another devastating miscarriage, but something inside told her she wouldn't. That the foundation she and Ras had created when their bodies met for those incredible expressions of togetherness would hold her womb strong, would protect the life growing within her.

Ever the realist, she had expectations of what Ras would do once he heard the news. Nothing. After all, what could he do? He was obligated to marry Vajhana, and together they would breed a proper successor to the throne. It was the approved alignment of stars in the sky. It was what was right.

Gracie understood that. Yes, it would be a perfect universe if she and Ras could be together, could raise their miracle as a couple in love. Just like his parents did before his mother tragically died. She'd never known the love of a family and still wouldn't. That tightness of a unit that, surrounded by love, looked out for one another. And shared private joys. Once again that was not her lot. She was destined to be left behind. But in this case the consolation was a magnificent gift.

Yet she couldn't not tell him about it, couldn't hold the secret within her for the rest of her, and her baby's, life. Ras was entitled to know he'd be a father. She assumed he would not want, or be able, to have anything to do with her. That he couldn't, wouldn't, shouldn't ever even meet the baby. As years went by, she'd explain the blessing as being assisted by a sperm donor who had sold his seed for money and had no interest in knowing the results of his actions. Women did that all the time.

The irony, of course, was that Gracie never thought she'd get pregnant again. Never thought she'd want to. She'd considered it, but had never really seen herself going through with it. She was supposed to be alone in every way. Not taking any chances. Yet it turned out she could hardly have felt more opposite. She was filled with nothing but optimism and glory. She had Ras's baby inside her! Who already had a personality. She didn't know the gender, but he or she was someone Gracie already knew. Because the fetus inside her was half Ras. Every cell in her body recognized the new life as belonging to love. If she couldn't have him, at least she could have his child.

She loved Ras so much that she was more than willing, ecstatic, to bring his baby into the world. Even if no one ever knew who his or her father was. Because that little human was going to be as magnificent, as strong and noble and intelligent as Ras. It would be her honor to raise this child who would bring good wherever he or she went, bring magic to anything she or he touched. It was a brand-new day.

And she wanted Ras to know all of that. So she tapped the phone number that he had given her. If after she gave him the news he asked her to keep the number in case she or the child were ever in dire need, she would. But she'd vow never to use it.

The phone rang three times before she heard the recipient's click. "Hello."

"Ras?"

"Gracie?"

"Yes."

"I can't believe it's you. I was going to call you today."

Hmm, Gracie couldn't imagine why, although he'd taken her phone number as well. They'd left nothing unsaid. The teary farewell at the airplane hangar in New York was about as final as anything could be, with them basically wishing each other a sweet life. Spent apart.

"I have to tell you something, Ras."

"Are you okay?"

"More than okay."

"Me first, then. I love you." His voice was like gold. In the very center of her, she glistened at hearing that he loved her. The words made her eyelashes flutter. She stroked the tiny basket in her hand with the pad of her thumb.

"I love you, too."

"I have to see you."

"I… I don't think that's a good idea."

"I have to be with you."

"What are you saying, Ras?"

"Can you come to Ko Pha Lano? I'll send a plane."

"Ras, what about your fiancée? Your father?"

"I can't live a life that isn't mine."

"Your subjects need…"

"Our citizens remember my mother. They remember a time at the palace when her zest touched everyone. They will return to that with you here, Gracie."

Alone in her Boston hotel room she shook her head without anyone to see it. "It can't be, Ras."

"It can be. It will be. I don't want to clip your

independence. You can be free to pursue anything you want to, my love. We, and the people, will work it out. In fact, I think you might be interested in an idea that I want to talk to you about. In person."

"I have something I need to tell you, too."

"Save it for *in person*. I can't wait to hear it." That remained to be seen. Would he regard the baby as good news? A pregnant American suddenly on the prince's arm when he was engaged to be married in mere weeks.

"But…"

"But what?"

"I…" Was she going to protest, when the man she adored had confessed his love for her?

"Get to the airport."

This wasn't possible, wasn't supposed to be. She literally pinched her arm to make sure she hadn't fallen into what just had to be a beautiful dream. After all they'd been through, all the while knowing their ultimate destinies had already decided their outcomes, it couldn't end with her getting the prince. Could it?

Ras could hardly believe it when he watched the love of his life descend on the plane that had transported her to his home. He rushed to meet her on the tarmac. The wrenching farewell that he'd thought was permanent had changed course!

"Gracie, Gracie, Gracie..." Saying her name took turns with kisses delivered all over her face. He took her by the hand and led her to the waiting car. In the back seat he turned to look into her eyes. "You're here."

"I am, Ras. As the plane was landing, I was amazed at all of the natural beauty of the island and the clear blue of the water. I can see why you feel so protective of it."

Once they arrived at the palace, he ushered her into a salon where they could talk. He saw her touch her stomach, that habit she had been working on breaking. "Are you nervous?" he asked, gesturing to her motion.

"I am. That's not all. There's a reason I've been instinctively cradling my belly lately. A reason I hope you'll be happy about."

Her words were an explosion as he interpreted their meaning. "Are you saying you're..."

"Yes, my love. I'm pregnant. I don't know what kind of chaos that might wreak, so I haven't told anyone."

"Chaos? That's the most beautiful news I have ever heard." He swallowed hard, overcome with emotion. "I'm the father of your child!" He rushed closer to touch her belly, which, now that he noticed, actually did feel a tiny bit rounded.

"It's too early to sense any motion."

He caressed her over and over nonetheless. "No. I can feel him or her. I'm sure of it." She laughed, music to his ears. "Do you realize you're carrying the future king or queen?"

"I am acutely aware of that," she said, smiling. "It's quite nerve-racking. Especially after…"

"We'll get you the finest doctors. And we won't make any announcements right away." He bounced in his boots as he hugged her, then brought her to a chair to sit down, then kissed her cheek, then went to pour her a glass of water. "I'm giddy. Thank you, Gracie. Thank you for the most amazing miracle anyone could receive."

"But what about your obligations? Princess Vajhana? The partnership of the two islands? The manufacturing development?"

"I've already broken things off with her. That's why it was such perfect timing when you called. I was just going to call you. To make arrangements. Because it's you I'm going to spend the rest of my life with."

"What did she say? What did your father say?"

He explained that Vajhana was in Dubai when

he'd reached her. That she'd said she was relieved because she didn't want to get married yet. Apparently, the freedom quest Ras was on in the States with Gracie wasn't anything compared to the wild oats Vajhana still needed to sow. And Ras had explained to Gracie about convincing his father that being with the woman he loved was to everyone's benefit. "I had help from a four-legged friend."

That night, Gracie met Lucky Two and His Majesty King Maho. She became fast friends with them both, as Ras knew she would. Over dinner, he told the king that he was to be a grandfather. The grin that cracked over his face made him look fifteen years younger. "Well done, Gracie," the king said, nodding to her.

"And I wanted to talk to both of you about something else, so I'm very delighted to have you at the same table." He retrieved the laptop he'd put on a side cupboard before dinner. "Father as you know, when we were to partner with King Yodfa and the people of Ko Yaolum, I was against anything that might rob the island of its resources. I believe this is what's best for our nation," he said firmly while showing them the prospectus he had been working on, essentially for years.

"Hmm." The king let out a sound of interest that encouraged Ras.

"Then you'll consider it, Father?"

"I can see you've done a lot of research. I have a number of questions about the feasibility."

"I promise you I have all the answers. And Gracie is a licensed travel consultant with an endless supply of good ideas. I want her to be one of the creators of our program. Will you, Gracie? Will you help our island become all that it could be?"

"Of course! I'd love to!"

Ras wasn't finished. He stood from his dining chair and approached Gracie's. He got down on one knee and removed his mother's wedding ring from his jacket pocket where he had been touching it throughout dinner. Something must have told him that he would need it someday as he had never given it to Vajhana. He held it in his open palm. "Will you officially join our family and all that it entails? Will you marry me?"

"It will be my honor."

Bursting with elation, he slipped the ring onto her finger and they kissed. Then Gracie rose and went to the king's chair. He stood. She bowed her head and then hugged him. "Thank you," she said, knowing that without the king's approval none of this would be possible.

After a conversation that lasted late into the night, the four of them proceeded down the palace hallways toward their rooms. The king, the crown prince and his pregnant love continued to exchange thoughts, come to conclusions, energize with specifics. Alongside them Lucky Two romped, understanding the many meanings of his name.

* * * * *

If you enjoyed this story,
check out these other great reads
from Andrea Bolter

Caribbean Nights with the Tycoon
Wedding Date with the Billionaire
Captivated by Her Parisian Billionaire
His Convenient New York Bride

All available now!

up her mind where she wants everything to go. Hell, I'm glad I'm not her husband. She probably keeps him busy moving their household furniture around.''

Mike scratched his head and tried to look puzzled. ''Thought a Mr. Petrov was the boss. You know, a tall, thin dark-haired guy with a mustache?''

''Ain't seen anyone who looks like that around here this afternoon. Come on, let's get this bookcase down to the truck. They ain't paying us by the hour.''

Mike hoisted his end of the bookcase and took a quick look around before he backed out of the office. He'd have to get back up here and check out the other rooms for himself after the moving job was finished.

An hour later, Mike ended his covert survey of the office with an oath. If Petrov had ever been here, he wasn't here now.

He pulled out his cell phone to call Charlie to tell her he was on his way back. To his dismay, an operator told him that number was out of order. He remembered the telephone lines at Charlie's house had been cut and there hadn't been time to have them repaired. And, worse luck, he didn't know her cell phone number!

He was one hell of a bodyguard to have let that critical fact get away from him, he cursed himself as he ran for his car. He jumped in and headed out on the Beltway just as dusk was falling. His sixth sense told him he had to get back to Charlie before darkness fell.

As ORDERED, Charlie locked the kitchen door behind Mike. She leaned her head against the closed door and forced herself not to fling it open and beg Mike to stay with her.

Several deep breaths later, she gazed apprehensively around her. Every shadow, the heavy silence, even the idea of darkened rooms beyond the kitchen seemed intimidating.

It was all Mike's fault. She'd been hanging around him too long, she thought as she shivered at the pictures her imagination conjured up. She reminded herself she was at home with the doors and windows locked.

She'd make coffee, strong, black coffee, she decided. Something to do to keep from worrying about Mike and the danger he might be in. She grabbed a package of coffee out of the refrigerator, found the grinder, put in two tablespoons of coffee beans and pressed the button. The smell of freshly ground coffee filled the room, but even that didn't help.

Suddenly exhausted by waiting for the unknown, Charlie folded her arms and put her head down on the table. Only for a moment. Only for a moment before she made herself a sandwich, she told herself before she drifted off to sleep.

A sound awakened Charlie. She gazed around the

kitchen—she was alone. Instinct sent her to the closet where the flashlights were stored. She grabbed one to use as a weapon, just in case, tiptoed to the dark hallway and peered into the darkness.

No lights, she told herself. If there *were* someone in here with her, she knew the house better than an intruder did. She could have made her way around blindfolded.

She slowly inched her way down the hall to her bedroom and replaced the flashlight with the handgun she kept in her nightstand. She hated guns, but for the first time she felt grateful for the rudimentary security training course required of all State Department employees. She'd shoot to defend herself. She'd only use the gun if she had to.

What really bothered her was that if what Mike had finally told her about the threatening letters was true, she just might have to shoot. After what had happened to Liz, she didn't intend to give up without a fight.

Her cautious search of the house unfruitful, Charlie barricaded herself in the kitchen and prayed Mike would come back soon.

MIKE DROVE like a madman back to Charlie's house. If he were pulled over for speeding, at least he'd have a police escort and backup.

One half mile from her house, he saw a dark green Suburban parked off the road. Since there were no other homes on the road where Charlie lived, the car was either disabled or someone didn't want it to be seen.

Considering the circumstances, he strongly suspected the latter. Maybe the someone knew Charlie was alone.

Petrov!

Mike cut the car lights and coasted the rest of the way to Charlie's. With the exception of the kitchen lights, the house was dark. A light in the window for him to come home to? The idea sent a momentary warmth through him—until he remembered the abandoned car.

He drew his gun. He didn't have to check to see if it was loaded. It was. Carrying a gun wasn't a game to him—he played for real and for keeps.

Mike edged his way to the side of the house, faded into the shadow of a tall green hedge and waited for his eyes to become accustomed to the darkness. If there was someone out there, he was bound to make himself known sooner or later.

His heart pounding, his teeth on edge, he froze. Waiting was the part of the job he hated. Compared to waiting for the unknown, any action, especially if it meant catching Petrov, would be a piece of cake.

An eternity later, he finally spotted a tall, dark figure making its way around the corner of the house. The intruder stopped to check a window, then another, before it paused and turned to the kitchen door.

Mike relaxed. Thank God he'd remembered to check all the windows before he left for D.C. Now, all he had to worry about was the intruder's access to the kitchen.

"Charlie," he whispered. "Hang on, love, I'm coming."

The intruder reached the door. Silhouetted against the dim light was a man with what looked like a crowbar in his hand. The man, judging from Charlie and Liz's descriptions, must be Petrov. Mike's blood ran cold at the malevolent look he caught on the man's face when the kitchen light hit it. If ever he'd thought he could talk his way through the coming encounter, the thought vanished. It was the face of a man out to kill. Mike drew his gun.

"Petrov! Hold it right there!" Mike shouted, his gun aimed squarely at a spot between the man's eyes.

At the sound of Mike's voice, the man swung around and threw the crowbar he held in his hand straight at Mike.

Mike ducked. While there was still time to catch Petrov, he threw himself at the man. Caught off balance, Petrov tumbled to the ground and took Mike with him. They rolled over and over until, luckily, Mike found himself on top. Before Petrov could move, Mike caught the man's head between his hands and held him immobile. Blood ran from Petrov's nose.

"What are you doing here?" Mike said tersely. "And why?"

Petrov clamped his lips shut. To Mike's disgust, it was clear the man had no intention of answering questions.

Mike reached in his back pocket for handcuffs before he realized he was still wearing the moving company's jumpsuit. The handcuffs were back in his suit pants somewhere in D.C.

He stared down at Petrov and repeated his questions. "What are you doing here? Who sent you?"

Still no answer.

Without the handcuffs, there was only one way Mike knew to keep his captive quiet until help arrived. It wasn't like him, nor was it his usual method of operation, but Petrov's capture had become a case of use a gun or his fist. He pulled back his arm, balled his fist, and aimed for Petrov's left eye.

INSIDE THE HOUSE, Charlie heard shouts. She peered out a window just in time to see a man rear back and strike a figure on the ground. It was too dark to make out the figures clearly, but her heart jumped at the possibility the top figure could be Mike. What *was* obvious was that the person on the ground had no intention of giving up easily. The outcome of the fight was clearly up to her.

Charlie grabbed her gun, checked to see if it was loaded and unlocked the kitchen door. "Who's there?"

The figures on the ground erupted in a tangle of flailing limbs and cuss words.

"Stop, or I'll shoot!" Charlie shouted. "I'll do it," she added grimly when the figures untangled themselves. She was on her own. She bit back an oath, took a firm grip on the gun, tightened her finger on the trigger, closed her eyes and shot. The first man to head for her was a dead man—provided she hit him.

Simultaneously, two more shots rang out. To her dismay, both men lay motionless. She crept toward the nearest figure and turned him over. It was the face of the mysterious Blair House shooter. The missing man Mike had theorized was behind the threatening letters that named her as a target.

Suddenly sure the second figure was Mike, Charlie crept over to him. It *was* Mike! Oh, my God, she thought as she dropped the gun. She'd shot the man she loved!

Chapter Fourteen

For the second time in as many days, an ambulance pulled out of Charlie's driveway. Sergeant Hawkins, his suspicious eyes boring into Charlie, shoved his little black notebook in his pocket, capped his pen and threw up his arms.

"You sure lead an exciting life, Miss Norris," he said dryly. He motioned to the three handguns his assistant had tagged and placed into separate plastic bags. "I'll have to ask you to run both shootings by me one more time, but it looks as if you've been telling the truth all along." He glanced at the guns and grimaced. "But did you have to shoot both of them? All you had to do was call me. I would have taken care of your visitors—without all this blood."

Charlie stared at the two separate puddles of blood on the driveway—one Mike's, the other Petrov's—and shuddered. She didn't have the strength to tell Hawkins one of the injured men was the man she loved. Or that she'd been too busy trying to stay alive to use her cell phone. He was in no mood to believe her.

"I distinctly remember firing only once, Sergeant," she managed. "I'm not even sure which man I shot."

Hawkins grinned. "We'll find out soon enough. In the meantime, I'll call it a matter of shooting in self-defense. Oh, by the way, I almost forgot to mention that we found your uh…kangaroo."

Charlie acknowledged what seemed to be the only good news of the day. She'd almost burst into tears at the sight of an unconscious Mike on a gurney being thrust into the ambulance. To make matters more hurtful, she hadn't been allowed to go to the hospital with Mike because Petrov was in the ambulance with him. Hawkins hadn't said so, but she had a strong suspicion he didn't trust her to be alone in the ambulance with the men.

Charlie wiped the tears from her eyes. She'd had enough. More than enough. She couldn't recognize herself as the woman who'd actually shot and injured someone. The change in her frightened her. She'd always considered herself as strong as a rock, but obviously even a rock could break.

The answer was heartbreakingly clear. She couldn't go on living this way; not knowing from one moment to the next if Mike was in danger. Or worse, if he was alive.

Giving Mike up wouldn't be easy, but she knew

she had to. She hated guns and violence, yet she'd actually shot someone tonight. To her everlasting torment, that someone could be Mike.

She'd changed all right. But, if shooting came as part of her new persona, she didn't want any part of it.

BY THE TIME Charlie finally reached the hospital the next morning, she'd steeled herself to say goodbye to Mike. To tell him she couldn't live the type of life he offered.

To her dismay, Mike's hospital room was full. Wade and his duchess were there. Even Sergeant Hawkins, looking official in his dress uniform, was in attendance.

"Charlie!" The duchess rushed to hug her. "Mike told us what happened! You are so brave! Are you all right?"

Over the duchess's shoulder, Charlie felt Mike's eyes on her. Outwardly, he looked calm, but she sensed he must somehow have known why she was here. She forced a smile. "I'm fine, thanks."

"Are you sure? Sergeant Hawkins told us you shot Petrov!"

"Petrov?" Charlie's heart skipped. Part of the guilt she'd felt at having shot Mike lightened, but still some of it remained. She'd actually shot someone when every ounce of her being cried out against violence.

"Yeah," Hawkins broke in. "Ballistic tests matched the bullet that put Petrov down to your gun. But not before the guy shot Wheeler in the shoulder."

For the first time since the shooting, Charlie found she could breathe easily without feeling a lump in her throat. She might have been guilty of shooting Petrov, but thank goodness she hadn't been the one to shoot Mike!

Hawkins grinned at Mike. "Lucky for you the bullet hit you in your shoulder. It missed your heart by a couple of inches. *Your* bullet hit the kitchen doorjamb, or we would never have found it.

"By the way," Hawkins went on, "this fellow Petrov was so grateful to be alive he confessed to everything. Said he was the second shooter in the recent Blair House incident. Seems he was trying to create a diversion to keep some new Baronovian Embassy from opening."

"Yes," the duchess added. "When the Baronovia trade office closes and our new embassy opens, Petrov will not be able to continue to use the office in his marketing scheme."

"We had someone check the trade office records. They indicate he was at the head of a scheme that's made him a wealthy man," her husband added. "Guess he planned a last hurrah."

"Was he badly hurt?" Charlie gazed anxiously at Sergeant Hawkins. "The last thing I intended to do was to injure anyone seriously. I only wanted to break up a fight.''

She heard Mike clear his throat in the background. A reminder not to say too much? ''Oh, and yes. To defend myself.''

Hawkins laughed. ''Your aim was a little off the mark. He's a damn lucky guy. Looks like he's going to recover with just a scar on his chin.''

Mike broke in. ''Is he here at the hospital?''

''No. We released him on his own recognizance after he claimed diplomatic immunity.'' Hawkins shrugged. ''I asked him to keep the D.C. police posted as to his whereabouts, but…''

Wade Stevens, in his navy-blue uniform with three rows of gold braid on each sleeve, stood up and growled. ''We'll see about that! May?''

Stevens's bride smiled complacently. ''Not any more, Sergeant Hawkins. You have my permission to arrest Petrov at once.''

Hawkins frowned at her. ''About that, who did you say you are?''

Wade Stevens grinned and put his arm around his bride. ''Sergeant, meet the duchess Mary Louise of Baronovia, my wife.''

Hawkins gaped at the duchess. ''You've got to be kidding. Right?''

May waved her royal hand in dismissal. ''Go. Arrest Petrov at once.''

Hawkins snapped his little black notebook shut.

"I'm out of here. Guess I've got me a criminal to catch."

Stevens took his wife by the hand. "And we have a honeymoon to catch up on." He glanced pointedly at Charlie then grinned at Mike. "Looks as if you're in good hands now, Mike. Let me know if there's anything else May or I can do for you."

Finally alone with Mike, Charlie stepped to the bed where he lay, clearly exhausted, against his pillows. She had to force herself not to touch him, to clear his hair away from his damp forehead. "Are you really okay?"

Mike smiled weakly. "As good as a guy with a bullet hole in him can be. How about you?"

"I'm fine," she answered. Physically. Mentally, she was in torment. "I came to say goodbye, Mike," she said softly, "and to tell you how sorry I am to have caused you so much trouble."

"It's all part of the job," Mike said, "but I don't want your apologies, Charlie." He reached for her hand and rubbed it against his cheek. "If anyone should apologize for what happened, it's me. You have nothing to apologize for."

His deep, throaty voice broke the ice around Charlie's heart. Tears formed behind her eyes. How could she love this man with every ounce of her being and still have to leave him? "If you don't want my apologies, what do you want?"

"You, sweetheart. I want you to forgive me for

leaving you alone to fend for yourself. For not preventing Petrov from coming after you. And for driving you to use a gun. I never intended for matters to get that far.'' He grasped her hand in his. ''What do you say to starting over again?''

Charlie shook her hand loose. ''I'm sorry, I can't.''

''You can. You must love me, or you wouldn't keep knocking me down so I can't get away from you,'' he said with a hopeful smile. He searched her eyes with a longing that almost broke her resolve to leave him.

Charlie's heart twisted at Mike's attempt to make her laugh. ''I'm sorry, Mike. I've seen what love can do to a woman,'' she went on. ''I can forgive you for having to leave me for some assignment. It's your job. What I can't bring myself to forget is that one day I might have to hear you were hurt in the line of duty. Or worse, killed. I almost hurt you myself.''

Sadness replaced the light in Mike's eyes. ''I hear you, sweetheart, but I find it hard to accept. Isn't there anything I can say to make you change your mind?''

Charlie shook her head and backed away from the bed. She had to leave before she threw herself into Mike's arms and into an unknown and perhaps dangerous future.

Mike held out a hand to her. "Before you go, I'd at least like to know if you ever really loved me."

Before Charlie could answer, a little figure burst into the room and threw himself on the bed. "Daddy! Daddy! Grandma says you were hurted. Can I see it?"

Mike's mother rushed into the room, breathless from trying to catch up with her little grandson. "Oh dear, I'm so sorry, Mike. I tried to tell Jake to take it easy, but…" Mike clasped Jake under his good arm. "The show-and-tell will have to wait," he told Jake. "Mom, I'd like you to meet Charlie Norris. Charlie, this is my mother, Minna."

Minna Wheeler's eyes lit up. "*The* Charlie?" Mike nodded. "I'm so happy to meet you, Charlie," his mother answered. "Mike has spoken about you."

"I want to see your hurt, Daddy!"

Mike laughed. "First, how about saying hello to Charlie Norris."

Jake squirmed in his father's arms. "Hi, Miss Charlie! Are you hurted, too?"

Charlie's aching heart went out to the motherless little boy. She'd grown up taking care of her three younger siblings, had even thought she'd had enough of small children to last her a lifetime, but Jake was different. Of course, she thought, as she smiled at the picture he and his father made against the stark white hospital sheets, he was different from most children. He was Mike's son.

"No, I wasn't hurt," she said, smiling into the little boy's anxious eyes. "I just came to say good-bye to your father."

"But not before you answer my question," Mike interrupted quietly. Over Charlie's frantic signal of objection, he want on. "I have to know if what was between us was real or just a game."

"What kind of game, Daddy?" Jake asked. "What do you want Miss Charlie to tell you, Daddy?"

Mike's eyes challenged Charlie to answer his question.

For a long moment, Charlie was unable to speak. How could she tell Mike she'd fallen in love with him almost from the first time she'd tripped him and fallen on top of him? How could she tell him she would never be able to forget his smile, the sound of his voice? Or the strong arms that held her when he'd kissed her? Or when he'd made love to her?

She finally cleared her throat. "Your father wanted to know if I love him."

Jake eyed her curiously. "You do, don't you, Miss Charlie?"

"I'm afraid I do," she answered, her gaze locked with Mike's, her heart pounding in a rush of love. "I'm afraid I do."

Jake crawled across the bed and reached up to

grab Charlie's hand. In the background, she heard Mike's mother's gasp of pleasure.

"Don't be afraid, Miss Charlie. Daddy's good at taking care of people," he assured her. "I am, too. We'll both take care of you."

And, to Charlie's everlasting daily delight, they did.

Epilogue

For years after Charlie Norris and Mike Wheeler got married in a special wedding at Blair House, people spoke of their wedding. Where else, they would ask, have you ever seen a wedding where a little kangaroo with a black tie around its neck was a member of the bridal party?

How to Marry A HARDISON

by Kara Lennox

continues this December in

HARLEQUIN®

AMERICAN *Romance*®

SASSY CINDERELLA

After an accident knocked him off his feet,
single dad Jonathan Hardison was forced to hire
a nurse to care for him and his children.
The rugged rancher had expected a sturdy,
mature woman—not Sherry McCormick,
the sassy spitfire who made Jonathan wish
their relationship was less than *professional*....

**First you tempt him.
Then you tame him...
all the way to the altar.**

Don't miss the other titles in this series:

VIXEN IN DISGUISE
August 2002

PLAIN JANE'S PLAN
October 2002

HARLEQUIN®
Makes any time special ®

Visit us at www.eHarlequin.com   HARHTMAH3

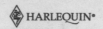

Steeple Hill Books is proud to present
a beautiful and contemporary new look
for Love Inspired!

HEARTWARMING INSPIRATIONAL ROMANCE

Love Inspired.

As always, Love Inspired delivers
endearing romances full of hope, faith and love.

Beginning January 2003
look for these titles
and three more each month
at your favorite retail outlet.

Steeple
Hill®

Visit us at www.steeplehill.com

LINEW03

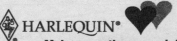

Coming in December from

HARLEQUIN®

AMERICAN *Romance*®

and

Judy Christenberry

RANDALL WEDDING
HAR #950

Cantankerous loner Russ Randall simply didn't need
the aggravation of playing hero to a stranded
Isabella Paloni and her adorable toddler. Yet the
code of honor held by all Randall men wouldn't
allow him to do anything less than protect
this mother and child—even marry Isabella
to secure her future.

**Don't miss this heartwarming addition
to the series**

Brides
for Brothers

Available wherever Harlequin books are sold.

HARLEQUIN®
Makes any time special®

Visit us at www.eHarlequin.com

HARR